Savage Island

A **BREATH** NOVEL

Savage Island

VICTORIA DOUGHERTY

Savage
Island

Text copyright ©2018 by Victoria Dougherty

Cover design by Brianna Harden, www.briannaharden.com
Typesetting by Chris Bell, Atthis Arts, www.atthisarts.com

Published by Bloodwilde Press
Printed in the USA

ISBN (hardcover)   978-1-955039-00-0
      (paperback)   978-1-7342234-0-8
      (ebook)   978-0-9974657-7-8

Visit the author at www.victoriadoughertybooks.com

"*I am confident that there truly is such a thing as living again, that the living spring from the dead, and that the souls of the dead are in existence.*"

—*Socrates*

Chapter 1

Niue, 1944.

ON THE ISLAND of Niue, it's hard to believe the whole world is at war. The sky is as blue as Aunt Kitty's eyeshadow, and whale song erupts any old time from the flat plain of ocean surrounding us. Those giant doves of the sea, cooing at us like gods of an ancient world. "You're not of this earth," they seem to say. "You're one of us now."

One of us. No bloody way. And I never will be. No matter how long mum makes us stay here.

I mean, really—look at this place. Matapa Chasm, carved out by the sea—its porous rock walls, dark as cigarette ash—will remain safe and remote no matter how many people die in Europe and the Orient.

I've got no doubt the villagers will still trickle in in here for an afternoon swim even if Hitler and Hirohito have their way. Just as they do now. Right there's the plump-bottomed woman who works at the post office. White perfectly square teeth with a big space between the front two—she smiles at me and waves before beginning to untie her beach dress, revealing a pale pink bathing suit that makes her breasts look enormous. Everyone's been very welcoming, I have to give them that. And they have every reason to be. The fresh, cool waters will beckon these islanders just as they did the ancient kings of this place centuries ago. Toes will dip daintily into the crystalline waters, as my toe is doing right now.

"Come for a swim," the waters will say. No need to whisper. We're far, far away and nobody will hear. Certainly not the dreaded Axis.

"Angelie!"

It's Mum.

"I'm coming!"

"Lunch is ready! Fish."

What else?

"Don't want it to get cold!"

That's Aunt Kitty, Mum's twin. Aunt Kitty's always afraid of things getting cold. Sandwiches, in her estimation, can get too cold. So can potato salad.

I trudge carefully over the craggy swells of rock, picking my shoes up off of Donald Duck, a rather big hunk of million-year-old coral that's formed in the shape of Mum's favorite Disney character. A sign, she says, that we made the right choice in coming here. I remind her there was no "we" about it. This was entirely her idea. Aunt Kitty came along because what else was she supposed to do? We're all she's got.

"I saw one of those lion fish," I tell them.

Kitty gasps. "In the chasm?" Her eyes dart over to the pool, as she spreads a tablecloth over the flat bed of rock that's going to serve as our table.

"In a coral pool near the arches."

Kitty shakes her head while Mum serves the fish onto banana leaves, careful the filets don't break apart.

"Those are poisonous, Angelie!" Kitty says with another quiver.

"Venemous," I say. "And not at all deadly. Even if one of them had poked me, the worst that would happen is my foot would swell up."

The lion fish are like everything on Niue. Beautiful, yet with a murderous appearance.

"And don't you go climbing around those Arches of Talava again, oh my word. Anyone can see you from above!" Kitty warns.

Now the very sky has become a danger. See, two days ago – only a week after our unceremonious arrival on this rock – a V formation flew high over Alofi Bay. Only they weren't birds. Mum trained her binoculars on them and recognized the markings.

"God Save the Queen!" Aunt Kitty called up to the sky, waving her yellow cotton handkerchief. The one she cried into all the way on the journey from Sydney—wringing it over the railing—her tears dispersing into the ocean brew.

"They're Yanks," Mum announced, passing the binoculars to her.

"They're Allies," Kitty countered.

Ever since, word has spread and there's nothing but talk of the war. And that's all it is. Talk, talk, talk. What else is there to do here?

"Those things are sharp all over and a good wind can come and blow you right off the top."

Aunt Kitty's still on the damned Arches of Talava.

"You know they used to call this place *Savage Island*. For years and years, they did, oh my word!" Aunt Kitty bites into a flaky chunk of parrotfish and her eyes bulge. She pulls a thin, white bone out of her mouth as if it's proof of the hidden perils that surround us.

"They only called it Savage Island because of Captain Cook," Mum says, laughing. "I imagine that, from his perspective, it was rather accurate, but it's a good lesson not to judge things by the way they look."

The islanders drove him off three times back in the

1770s—they're very proud of that here and take every chance to tell you about how they painted their teeth a bloody scarlet with skins of red banana, and jumped and screamed to all insanity. You know, like *savages*. Cook could see them up close, as his ship was only fifty feet or so from the beach. Deep water there. We're on a rock after all, and the short shelf of coral reef drops off into a blue as deep as the Queen's sapphire.

Last even remotely interesting thing that's happened here.

"Savage Island. Hard to believe Nuie was ever called that," I say.

Mum tisk-tisks me.

"Angelie, we're in a lovely place far away from the war. You heard what Sister Mary Frances told us back home. People need us on this island—for Christian fellowship. And you can put your gardening to use. So many of the home gardens here are a pity, what with all the coral and sandy soil about."

"You can make anything grow, oh my word," Kitty says. "Thumb as green as your eyes."

I'm *this* close to rolling my eyes.

"We're on a rock and everyone here seems to have been doing just fine without us. The people who need us are trying to keep the whole world from being consumed by evil!"

I give one big huff and Mum kisses the top of my head.

"Strawberry blonde, but all strawberry in temperament. Just like your dad." She nudges me to eat my fish. "And we've given our share to the war effort."

I pinch a piece of fish and place it on my tongue. Delicious. Fresh and salted. A hint of coconut. I tell Mum how good it is, since I feel like such a rat.

By "our share," Mum means my brother and father. They died nearly two years ago now. Jay on a merchant ship sunk by a Japanese submarine, and Dad in the attack on Sydney Harbor. Although there have been no attacks since, and boats like the ones Dad and Jay went down on have by and large managed to keep away from the likes of the enemy, most of Sydney has been sure that at any time the Emperor himself will show up at their very front doors with two samurai, lop off their heads, and bring them back to Tokyo as souvenirs!

"What's that?" Aunt Kitty asks. She stands, her freckled nose tipped up and pointing out to sea.

Mum turns around and squints her eyes. "A barge, I think."

"I thought those only come once a month," I say. That last one came a day or so after we arrived.

Mum shrugs. "There was a big hullabaloo at the post office today, that's all I know. A man named Max Vogel is coming to the island."

"Vogel," I say. "A German?"

Mum nods.

"At least he's not a Jap!" Aunt Kitty crosses herself. "But still, what's a German doing here?"

Mum takes a serving of bread fruit, passing me a slice. "That's what everyone wants to know."

"Well, damn the Germans," I say.

"Angelie, watch your mouth!"

Mum and Aunt Kitty say it in perfect unison, reminding me of the real reason we moved here. Mum thought I was starting to go wild back home, and saw my new fondness for the word damn as something akin to a leper spot. She thinks I've been clubbed by the crook deal we got from what happened to Dad and Jay and island life is sure to cure me.

"If we can't damn the Germans and the bloody Nips,

who can we damn," I tell them. At nearly seventeen I think I've got the right to swear.

"That's not the point," Mum says. "Only God can damn another soul."

Here we go again. "I thought we were instruments of the Lord."

Aunt Kitty sniffs. "Instruments, not bludgeons, darling."

Well, this instrument has every intention of finding out everything there is to know about Herr Max Vogel and what in the name of Saint John the Baptist he's doing here of all places. Not that I'm going to tell Mum that.

Chapter 2

ELBOW MY WAY around a group of islanders, all bunched up together and gaping out at the water like they're waiting for fireworks to start. The barge is closer now, lit up, a dozen or so lights marking its shape like a constellation. The Big Shipper.

And there's another boat. This one coming from the barge, illuminated by an unblinking eye of light beaming from its stern. Bullying white, it even outshines the image of a full moon reflected on the surface of the bottomless, black water just past the coral reef.

A bloke about my age starts to thump his palms on his *nafa*—bum-bu-bum-bu-bum—and the hair on my arms stands up. Son of the friendly woman from the post office, he's long limbed and built like he should be tall, though he's a fair bit shorter than me. His sister, can't remember her name either, stands next to him all plump and pretty. She's got a shock of curly black hair that hugs her skull like a bathing cap fixed with floppy rubber roses, and starts to sing *Haku Motu*. Out of tune.

"Welcome Max Vogel," I say, mostly to myself. "I'm sure you'd much prefer Deutschland Über Alles."

All around me there's whispers mixed up in English and Niuean, which is how most of the people on this rock talk.

"You want a coldie, Will?" I hear Mum say from behind

me. Half the blokes on the island are named Will. "Swan Lager that came in from the last barge." Leave it to her to bring refreshments.

Will, whoever he is, apparently does want one, and I hear the pop from the bottle cap as Mum opens the beer.

"*Fakaue*," says a soft voice, more man than boy. It's *thanks* in Niue. *Glug, glug, glug*, this Will must've drunk up half the beer in three seconds flat.

Ooooo. It comes in harmony from the folk around me as the boat comes up to shore and the front line of Niueans get a load of her passengers. I struggle forward, pushing through, and the first thing I see is a neat helmet of very blond hair—obviously blond even in the dim glow of torch-light. This hair is perched on top of a square and lean face with the prominent bones of a predatory bird. The body, of one Max Vogel I presume, is as upright as the pressed uniform of a general, and he is everything I've imagined a German to be and more. Except for the way he's dressed. A simple shirt and pants, light in color—maybe powder blue. Very casual, like he's come on vacation.

But that's not the strangest part.

With him is a man. Skin as dark as the night sky, the whites of his eyes like pearls. His clothes are not nearly as pale as Max Vogel's, and seem somehow more serious. He's crouched behind the German, his forearms balancing on his knees as if he's thinking deep and hard about something.

"*Fakaalofa lahu atu!*"

A young man, Niuean, but with his waist-length hair plaited in a long braid, walks into the shallows to greet the boat. Wet to his thighs, his linen shirt clings to his chest, the more it's splattered with the frothy spray of ocean water. The Niuean girls are all watching him like he's Frankie Sinatra.

"That's Will Tongahai," Aunt Kitty pants into my ear. I didn't know she'd come up behind me.

"Is he the one who returned from London a while back?"

Aunt Kitty nods. "From some fancy boarding school, oh my word. His mum told me he tried to join the Royal Navy to go fight in the war!"

The only person who's been talked about more than Captain Cook since our arrival on Niue is Will Tongahai. He's the grandson of missionaries from the London Missionary Society—darned Protestants, as Aunt Kitty likes to say—and his mother married Nukai Tongahai, who owns the biggest plantation on the island. It's always a huge deal when a native son leaves here for the big, wide world and comes back. He's treated as if he's returned from Mount Olympus and is half-god now or something.

And Will Tongahai, half-god—that is to say half-British, which is pretty much the same thing on Niue—is extending his hand to Max Vogel and the African bloke who's come with him. Will gives a pleasant nod to Vogel like the man's not even German!

"Cornelius Kandinsky Neville," I hear the African say.

What in the bloody hell kind of name is that?

This Neville chap scans the crowd and his eyes fix on me like I glow in the dark. Makes sense, I guess, as I'm only one of a handful of folks who are obviously not from here. Will Tongahai turns his head to see what Neville's looking at and his eyes find me, too. He smiles and I feel naked all of a sudden.

"Hello," I say.

"Hello." Will Tongahai and that Neville fellow say it overlapping each other like *Hello-ello*. Max Vogel says nothing, concentrating instead on stepping out of the boat without slipping on the carpet of coral on the reef. That

Neville is not nearly as careful. He swings his legs over the side and makes his way to me, each tread more sure than the last.

"Who have we here?" Neville says. "More English?"

"Australian," I say. "Sydney."

"Ah, I love Sydney. One of the great, but little known cities in the world." He speaks British English but with an accent I can't quite place.

"Not little known to Australians," I tell him.

He smiles all friendly, as if he finds my cheekiness cute or something. Will Tongahai comes up and his eyes brush my face like he expects me to look at him the way all of the girls here do, but there's no way I'm going to do that.

"What brings you to Niue?" I ask Neville. He glances over at Max Vogel who has now waded the few feet up to shore.

"Same thing that brought me to Sydney," he says.

"What's that?"

He reaches into a sharp-looking leather bag, expensive but well worn, and pulls out a little statue that's only a mite bigger than his hand when held out flat. It's got a bird's head and wings, the mouth of a lion with its teeth bared. Odd, but I kind of like it. Cornelius Kandinsky Neville tosses it up and catches it, gazing at it like a long-lost love.

"Archaeology," he says, pronouncing every syllable.

Chapter 3

ONE SIDE OF Will Tongahai's face is aglow in firelight. The other blends entirely into the night, making him look like a handsome ghoul. His thick, long braid of hair snakes over his shoulder and down past his breast. It's fairer than it looked at a bit of a distance. The color of raw honey, instead of the shiny black of most Niueans. But then he is half British. He looks out at the water, and then kicks at the rocky sand at our feet. The barge, barely visible now, is on its way back to the mainland and I'm jealous,

"Quite a change from Sydney," he says.

Will is tall, taller than me at any rate. My eyes look into the hollow at his throat.

"You been to Sydney?"

He shakes his head, and the torchlight flickers for a spell over the whole of his face.

"Then how would you know this is a change from Sydney?" I ask him.

"Well," he says. "Just a good look at you for one thing."

Will Tongahai turns on his heel and saunters towards Vogel and Neville, his broad shoulders barely sheathed by the worn, white linen of his shirt. He wears it that way on purpose, I guarantee it, and I feel sorry for the girls here who beg for his attention. Quite clear he's only interested in himself. There he is chatting up the men who could be the damned enemy for all we know. The three of them hover around Mum's drinks table, and I stride over, plucking a coldie from Mum's cooler.

"Angelie!" Aunt Kitty slaps my hand, making me give it back.

The three of them turn and Will Tongahai grins big as a moonslice.

"He got one," I say, pointing to *him*.

"He's nearly eighteen," Mum says, Aunt Kitty standing behind her, arms all folded in a *see, told you so* way.

"And so am I."

"A year from now!" Mum clarifies for everyone to hear. "Besides, he's a young man."

"Not old enough to join the Navy, I hear."

I can feel the three of them staring at me and that Neville bursts out laughing—a deep, throaty laugh that's all plush new velvet. My cheeks burn hot, because I know I shouldn't have said it. I mean, at least Will tried to join the war, and damned near would've succeeded if his roommate hadn't ratted him out, from what I hear.

Mum takes a deep breath and tells Aunt Kitty to go fetch a bottle of rum for Dr. Neville. So, it's Dr. Neville, is it? She uncaps the beer Aunt Kitty practically pried out of my hands and gives it back to me. I look her right in the eye as I take a long, deep swallow of the ale, which I hate and she knows it.

"Go set an example and sit down," she says, pointing at the tables she and the ladies have set up on the beach. "It's time to eat and everyone's just standing around."

I nod, heading towards a banquet flanked by long-stemmed torches with bulbous heads consumed in blue and orange flames. They're almost as bright as city streetlights and make the dining area the one place where you can actually see where you're stepping.

"You must be Angelie." A Niuean girl about my age comes up carrying two jugs of fruity wine.

"That's right," I say. I take one jug to help her out and wince. It's sticky and gums on to the front of my dress. "Great."

"Sorry about that," she says. She's got those big eyes like they all do here. "I'm Oliana."

"Angelie. Nice to meet you," I tell her. "At least it's not red wine, right?"

She giggles nervously and I give her my friendliest smile. We then take the jugs to a sideboard laid with palms and try to corral some of the elders into sitting down.

A *kai* feast has been thrown together in honor of our new guests. We got one of those, too, when we arrived, although this one looks a bit more . . . more, I have to say. I sit down at the head table—the longest one—and wait, my eyes grazing over all the varieties of roasted fish. They're surrounded by assorted preparations of taro, coconut, yam, and breadfruit. There's even some smoked ham and scary-ugly platters of giant coconut crab—alien things that Pacific Islanders are convinced ate Amelia Earhart after she crashed.

"That's why there was no sign of her," they say.

Those give me the creeps and I will not eat them, no matter how good Mum claims they are. Of course, Will Tongahai plops down next to me and picks one right up. He dislodges its abdominal sack—a thing filled with a thick, oily fluid—and goes to work slurping it down.

"It's good," he tells me. "Tastes like peanut butter."

I know it's impolite to grimace when someone's eating, but I can't help it. "Well, I've never had peanut butter."

"Hmm," he says. "Come to think of it, neither have I."

Oliana hovers near Will, clearly dying to take a seat next

to him. In the end she chickens out and takes the chair next to me.

Dr. Neville and Max Vogel sit directly across from us and I get up and serve them after a glowering look from Mum.

It's rather quiet on our end of the table as we start to eat. Clearly the travelers are starving. The other side of the table is all chitter-chat and that short-tall bloke plays his *nafa* in a low beat. He strums his fingers over the top of the drum, while shoveling food into his mouth with his other hand.

"You going to drink that?" Will says. I notice his beer has been empty for some time.

"I was, yes," I say. He waits as I lift up my beer and put it to my lips. Counting to three, I chug the whole thing down and place it back on the table with a thump. Will signals a local boy and asks him to bring us two more.

"Since you like it so much," he says.

Dr. Neville sits back and dabs his napkin at the corners of his mouth like he's some sort of gentleman. Max Vogel, on the other hand, places his elbows on the table. His banana blond hair is blown back by the same swift ocean breeze that makes the flames around us shudder.

"Kandi," he says to Neville in his short, German clip. "Mr. Tongahai tells me we can set up tomorrow morning. Claims the weather should be perfect all day."

By Mr. Tongahai, he must mean Will's father, the plantation owner.

"What are you setting up?" I ask.

Dr. Neville removes the statue from his bag again and places it on the table.

"You see this?" He says. "My father found it in a street market in Egypt. Paid almost nothing for it."

"Is it an Egyptian god of some sort?"

Neville smiles, his teeth as white as Chiclets. "It's not Egyptian at all. Much older."

"Sumerian?" Will Tongahai offers.

"Older even than that. At least that's what he believed."

I look the thing over, its strong thin body punctuated by an elegant pair of clawed feet clutching a flower. They look quite at odds with the way the head has been fashioned; that is all ferocity and intelligence.

"Like the essence of life itself," Will Tongahai says, as if picking the words from my mind.

"Correct, young Will."

"If you found it all the way in Egypt," I say, "then what's it got to do with here?"

Max Vogel chimes in. "It's carved from a type of rock that I am convinced exists deep beneath the desert floor in certain parts of the Sahara. Such a substance would be difficult to excavate under normal circumstances and quite impossible to access in these troubled times."

"And what, you think this substance could be found here, on Niue? We're all the way on the other side of the world."

"Ah, but we weren't once," Dr. Neville says. "Have you heard of the supercontinent?"

I shake my head.

"It's a theory that holds that all current land masses were once bonded together. That was over two hundred million years ago. Such a continent would have placed where we are right now rather close to the origins of the substance this strange little statue is made of."

I stroke my finger lightly on the statue's head and feel a slight shock, like when I used to touch the metal railing at our old house just after rubbing my feet over the rug.

"But Niue didn't exist back then," says Will Tongahai.

"Oh, it did," Max Vogel says. "It was much bigger, in fact. A real land mass. As this supercontinent broke apart, Niue was submerged into the Pacific. It broke the surface again many millions of years later when the volcano on top of which you now live became extinct and this coral atoll was formed."

Will Tongahai swigs his beer like it's water, and I feel a sick compulsion to do the same. No, in fact, I one up him and pretty much finish mine, ending with a burp that takes me by complete surprise. Dr. Neville and Will Tongahai bust up and I can't help but join them. Even Max Vogel allows the corners of his mouth to turn up just a little.

"So, you're here to find more of what this statue is made of?" I ask, suppressing more burps.

"Perhaps," Dr. Neville says. "We're here to take geological samples anyway. Dr. Vogel is one of the top geologists in the world, and he seems to think we have a decent shot."

He pets the head of his statue and, if I didn't know better, I'd swear the thing's been staring at me this whole time.

"May I?"

Dr. Neville hands the figure to me and I'm struck immediately by how warm it is. The heat from its core spreads from my hands into my wrists and up my arms, flooding my chest cavity like a gush of hot tea. All at once, I feel a searing pain in my face and my ribs, then my hips as if my bones have been broken by a series of heavy, wrathful blows. In the next twitch of time, the pain is gone as if it never was, and I'm left breathless.

"Are you alright?" I hear Will Tongahai say.

His words seem remote, like an echo.

Pinpoints of sweat break out all over me.

I start panting.

I can't speak.

It's as if my heart stopped and started again.

Everyone is looking at me.

I drop the statue on the table and rise up. Unable to manage any sensible excuses, I hurry off, tripping over the knobs of coral that pimple the way to the shore. Once there, I hobble along, arms out like airplane wings to keep balance, until I just can't go any more. I'm breathing so hard my head is spinning. In the distance, I see the Arches of Talava—two of them anyway—the moon shining on them like a reading light. The water hisses and sputters as it hits the rocky beach just a few feet away.

"Hey," I hear from behind me. "Hey, Angelie!"

I guess Will Tongahai knows my name.

He comes up next to me, his dark skin seeming blue in the alien glow of the island night.

"What is it?" he asks.

I glance up at his face and he's looking at me with real concern. I feel bad that I just up and ran away like that.

"I think I had too much to drink too quickly."

That smile of his again. "Impressive how you practically gulped the whole pint in one go. Took me some practice to get that good."

"Well, maybe I've had some practice, too."

"Hardly!" He says.

Now I want to wipe that smile off his face with the palm of my hand.

"What do you mean *hardly*?"

"I mean that until tonight you'd never had more than a sip of beer in your life, and that much you hated."

He crosses his hands over his chest and tips his head to his shoulder, as if weighing me.

"You know that do you?"

"Yeah."

"Well, I know you're a little prince on this island, and I bet a big city like London was a shock to you. So much competition." I practically spit out that last word.

"I was in Canterbury, actually."

"Oh, well, Canterbury then."

"You know what else I know?" Will steps closer and I clench my fists, planting my feet on the rough skin of the beach.

"Can't wait to hear," I say.

He drops his cheeky smirk and gets very serious all of a sudden. "You've never been kissed."

For a moment, he and I just stare one another down.

His eyes actually pierce the darkness even though they must be the color of mahogany. But I see these ribbons of amber curling around his pupils, and crimson threads as well. Sumptuous and royal. Damn they're beautiful. And damn him. He stands there, not at all backing down. Comfortable, immovable, like a Roman sculpture. While I feel as wayward as a mermaid. I don't know what makes me do it. A kind of fury, I guess. A low rumble of temper that starts like faraway thunder and grows. I veer towards him, taking his face in my hands. I press my small lips against his very plum ones, sweet and wet as if he's just licked them. And I do it hard.

Will lets me at first. Damn him, I even feel him grin while I kiss him. I'm about to push him away—I swear I am—when he takes the back of my head in his palm and brings me close in a deep, deep kiss that goes even deeper as he bends me back. It's not at all like I ever imagined being kissed. Not tender the way Humphrey Bogart kissed Ingrid Bergman in *Casablanca*. Will's kiss is wild. It's like the wind Aunt Kitty is so afraid might sweep me off the tops of the arches. The kind that blows my hair this way and that, scoops the breath right out of my rib cage. Every stroke of his tongue—on my lips, the roof of my mouth—is a star burst of sensations. Right when I think I can't take another moment, his hand slips down my neck and his hot breath drifts over my cheek as we pull apart. His eyes are incandescent, even this close, and they wander over my face like he's known me all my life.

Yes, I think to myself. Will Tongahai has most definitely kissed before.

I won't be fighting sleep tonight like I usually do, that's for sure. Trying to keep my eyes propped open to stop myself from going off into a dream world full of lunacy. Not after leaving Will Tongahai on the beach and trudging all the way back to the little thatched roof house in Hikutavake village. The one which, against my will (no pun intended), I now call home. Not after brushing my teeth with that awful charcoal powder mum traded for her old Timex watch. Replacing the taste of Will Tongahai with a bitter yuck that I deserve. Kissing him like that! What was I thinking?

"Angelie," he called after me when I started to go. I asked that he please not walk me home.

"Angelie!" My name sounds strange on his tongue. Like he should call me something else.

"You're a fast learner," he said. "That was one hell of a kiss."

I strip naked and lie on top of the covers of my cot. Soft and billowy. At least my covers are from home. The same ones from our bungalow in Burwood. My eyelids are as heavy as sopping wet towels. Just as well. I'd be up all night thinking about him anyway. How he smiled right onto my lips while I kissed him. The way he looked at me just as he leaned in for a second kiss. And I broke away—dropping him like I did that damned statue.

The statue the froggy-eyed man gave me. What was his name? Rin? No. Rin's not it. Neville. Neville gave me the statue. The African bloke. And his eyes aren't froggy at all. I'm dreaming. Must be. I'm in that in between place.

I see the statue laid out in a small pair of hands that are chapped and battered by the sun.

"What's it supposed to be?" I ask.

"Ah, a lady." It's the froggy man, again. Rin was his name. We're not here, on Niue, but in a desert. On a plateau looking out over an infinite sweep of sand.

"Hardly looks like a lady," I say. Doesn't sound like my voice, but it's me.

"What it looks like and what it is are not the same thing."

This Rin reaches out to me, then blows away like he's made of dust.

I'm on the other side now. Of sleep, of consciousness, of the universe.

I peel off from my body bit by bit, like a shave of beef from a sandwich. Sitting up first, then drifting towards the ceiling, looking down, watching my arms and legs settle into sleep. The way my creamy white skin looks so much like the salt dunes in the desert near where I was born. Not Sydney. Not our bungalow this time. My first home. My first life. In the same desert that made that statue.

Chapter 4

I**T'S LATE MORNING** and the sun is high and strong. We walk through waist-high stalks of taro plants, their leaves, cool and big as baby elephant ears, whooshing against us.

"They're near the drop-off," Oliana says.

I haven't been to the drop-off yet—the top of the steepest limestone cliffs that hug the coastline. And I don't much want to go today. Especially since I was conscripted by Rose Tongahai no less—Will's very mother—to bring lunch up to the Drs. Neville and Vogel.

They're there alright. But Will is nowhere in sight, thank God.

"*Fakaalofa atu!*" Oliana calls out.

Their heads are together about something and they step apart rather abruptly when they hear us. That Neville fellow, Kandi as the German calls him, gets all social all of a sudden.

"Well, hello, ladies," he says. "Nice to see you looking well, Miss Angelie. We worried about you last night."

Oliana looks down at her feet and I can see her begin to quiver with laughter. I give her my elbow. "I was fine, actually," I say. "Just a bit dizzy."

Kandi Neville is all scrutiny, but his smile remains a mask of casual cheerfulness.

"Good to hear," he says.

That Max Vogel mumbles something in German which Neville fully understands. He nods, answering back in that awful language and hands Vogel a little glass jar from his leather tote.

"What's that?" I ask.

"Specimen jar." He holds it up to the sun, allowing me to get a good look. "See, the glass is quite thick, making it impervious to breakage."

"Hmm," I say.

Neville is staring at me rather funny.

"Your eyes."

"My, granny, what big eyes you have," I say.

Neville chuckles. "I'm sure I'm not the first to notice them. They are a rather astonishing color."

No, he's not the first. They've been called everything from extravagant to spooky. "My eyes are green, Dr. Neville. That's not so odd for a fair-haired Aussie girl."

"No," he says. "But your eyes are no ordinary green, are they?"

I shrug.

"I once met a man with eyes that seemed to glow like a burning sunset."

I feel cold all at once. "Did you?" I say.

"Where was it, Max? In N'Djamena?"

"Ja." Max Vogel barely looks up from the sample he's scraping away from the limestone.

"You alright, Miss Angelie?" Neville asks. "You look pale."

I feel pale. Maybe the mention of sunsets. My dad used to take me to watch the sunset at Sydney Harbor. That was our time.

"Ah, Will, you're back. Speaking of curious peepers!"

I turn and see Will Tongahai coming towards us. I can

actually hear Oliana take in a breath—it's that loud and obvious—and make sure to temper my own reaction. Will seems to float over the taro leaves. He's wearing a beige jacket with lots of pockets and carrying a lumpy duffle bag that looks heavy.

"Hey, Will," I say.

He nods at me, then Oliana, and puts the duffle bag down. Sweating rather mightily, he strips down to his undershirt, revealing the most extraordinary tattoos—at least that's what I think they are—of flames licking up and down one of his arms. The other has the most glorious woman wrapped around it like a python. A rather ornate sheet of fabric hugs her body as if it's wet. Can't see her face as it disappears up his sleeve. As he bends down to unzip the bag, I see a blue blood moon on the nape of his neck. I've only ever seen tattoos on some of the blokes who worked on Jay's boat back in Sydney, and Will's are nothing like the boilerplate nautical images they had on their arms. Ships and squids and such. His are beautiful. Like works of art, and I can scarcely stop gaping at them. Will looks up and catches me red-handed, ogling him like an idiot. Instead of looking away, he keeps my gaze, as if daring me to wonder what the rest of him looks like.

"Do give a hand," Neville says, and Will unzips the duffle bag.

It's filled with picks and brushes, odd instruments that look vaguely medical—if you're a medieval doctor who practices on suspected witches, that is.

"What on earth are those?"

"My tool kit," Neville says.

"Should I run?"

The good doctor laughs and I rather like that he truly thinks I'm funny. Doesn't mean I trust him, though.

"Trowels and augers and mattocks," he says, pulling what looks like a giant corkscrew right out of the bag. "They do look rather sinister, don't they? But I assure you they're only used for digging and extracting precious, old objects. I've never once had to use them on a living person. Not yet, anyway."

Will Tongahai is awfully quiet. I glance back over at him and he's examining a thing that looks like a sickle, but with a long handle. In Will's hands, it seems more of a weapon than a tool, and it strikes me how natural he appears holding it.

"We brought you lunch," Oliana says, and Will points the tool at the ground, sharp-end down.

"Thank you," he says, taking her basket. "Won't you join us?"

Oliana jumps in with a yes before I can make our excuses. I curse myself for having worn a good dress—a lilac which I love and is one of my best, but not one that tries too hard, I hope. We all sit down on the rocky soil, and I have to tuck my dress under my knees. Certainly don't relish the thought of having to do more hand-wash tonight.

Will Tongahai passes me a sandwich smacking of smoked ham, and I swear he makes a point of brushing my fingers as he gives it to me. I pretend not to notice.

Oliana breaks open a coconut quite expertly, keeping its water trapped for drinking. She gives the first one to Will, of course. The next goes to Max Vogel, who grunts a *danke*, and then Kandi Neville. *Dr. Kandi Neville.* Then me.

"Niue," Dr. Neville says, holding up the big, green orb as if offering it to the gods.

"Behold the coconut." Will takes a healthy drink from his. "That's what Niue means."

"You're joking," I say.

Will shakes his head. "Better than Savage Island, don't you think?"

"Behold The Coconut is hardly a name to be proud of," I tell him. "At least Savage Island has some excitement to it."

"Is that what you're looking for—excitement?" Will slices several pieces of his coconut. They look like shards of the moon. He hands one to me.

"Not necessarily," I say. "But the name of an island should have something to it, don't you think? A good story, let's say."

Will leans back, resting on his elbow and crossing his feet at the ankles. His raw linen trousers inch up a bit and I see the pinkish-brown lines of more tattoo. Looks like the fleshy part of a palm, one from a delicate hand, that's resting lovingly on his ankle.

"A man could live on coconut," Will says. "You can drink from it, eat it, use it as a tool, even a missile." He takes the shell of his and chucks it at a tern perched up high on a palm. It squawks, cockles its feathers and flies off towards the shore. "Coconuts are survival on Niue. That tells a better story than scaring off the likes of Captain Cook."

"Ah, yes," Neville says. "Natural resources are the spine of a nation. Take my statue for instance—the one I showed you last night. There's a resource that's survived for millennia without so much as a scratch."

"Maybe it did," I say. "But the people who made it didn't."

Neville leans in to me, his breath soft and smelling of vanilla bean. "How do you know?"

"That statue looked terrifying to me," Oliana says. "With his big mouth and teeth."

"Maybe it's a lady," I say.

Neville turns to me and narrows his eyes. "What makes you say that?"

I shrug.

"Don't know. I had a dream about it last night is all. I try to write down my dreams. What I remember of them."

"So do I," Will says. "And I had a dream last night, too. About a sandstorm. That statue was there, I think."

"How awful," Oliana says.

Neville takes a bite of his sandwich and washes it down with coconut water. "You know, Angelie. The statue; she is a lady. At least that's what my father told me. The merchant who sold it to him said she was and relayed the most fascinating story about her. A bit of ancient folklore as it were."

"I'd love to hear it," I say.

"And I'd love to tell it, but I promised to do so tonight at the Tongahai's place, and I'd hate to ruin a good story by telling it twice."

Will sits up, dragging his finger through the soil. He draws a simple horizon with a sun or moon, I can't tell which.

"Won't you come," he asks me.

Oliana flits her eyes at me, looking disappointed.

"I couldn't," I say.

"But you must hear the story," Will says. "Especially after your dream."

"Your parents won't be expecting me."

Will shakes his head and Oliana looks back and forth between the two of us.

"I know they'd love to have you," he tells me. "Because they invited your mum, but your aunt is unwell, apparently. Perhaps she drank too much too quickly last night, too."

I glance up at Dr. Neville and he's staring at us, lips

pursed and eyes wide. Like we're one of the artifacts he's so enamored of. Max Vogel chortles, finding us oh so amusing or something, and I feel like a fool. Oliana wraps her arms around her knees.

"You should come," she says. "My family will be there."

Will is drawing in the dirt again. He leans back, allowing me a quick peek. *You were in my dream, too*, he writes. Then erases it.

The butterflies in my stomach are more like angry bees. I swallow hard.

"All right," I say. "I'll come."

Chapter 5

WILL'S HOUSE SITS on the edge of his property, its front windows staring big-eyed onto a sunset blushing over massive fields of taro, yams and tapioca. Their tree crops, made up of haphazard rows of mango, bananas, and coconut, are cultivated all the way behind the house in what looks like their very own private jungle.

The house itself is unlike the thatched-roof homes around the island. It's a modern house with sturdy cinderblock walls, a tin roof, and a generous wrap-around porch made of wood and painted a glossy, Oriental red. Impressive, yes, but unfussy, thank God.

There's a bonfire off to the side, and a roasting pit with one monster of a pig turning on the spit. Dr. Neville is near the fire at the center of the action—big surprise—and is flanked by Will, his parents, and two people who must be Oliana's mum and dad, by the looks of them. All round faces and strong bones.

"Welcome, Angelie!" Dr. Neville says, arms spread out. He takes a short bow.

Will Tongahai smiles, but makes no move at all. He stands there in a crisp shirt and trousers with his hair neatly plaited. As English as I've ever seen him.

"Thanks for having me."

"Lovely you could come, dear," says Rose Tongahai. She

looks me up and down like it's the first time she's seen me. "So pretty. Your mum make that dress?"

I glance down at my lilac dress, same one as before. I had to scrub the soil out of the skirt and hem and it's still damp in places. "Aunt Kitty did," I say. "She's a seamstress."

"And a good one, I see."

I like Rose. Mum sent me over to help her perk up her prized Kadupul flower the other day, and she was oh so nice, offering me tea and sandwiches while we tended to her drooping plant. A damned bugger of a thing, the Kadupul takes about a year to cultivate and even then blooms only once, and that's at midnight. The fragrance is heaven, but it's always dead by dawn, so I can't really see the point. Still, I ask her about it.

"Her leaves are crisp and green since you came by," she says. "I think she'll bloom any week now."

I tell her I think that's wonderful and turn to her husband.

"*Fakaalofa atu*, Mr. Tongahai."

Butchered that one.

"Angelie," he says, nodding.

Mr. Tongahai makes me a bit nervous. He seems nice enough, but there's never a wasted word with him.

"And these are the Vakaafis," Rose says.

Oliana's parents for sure, then.

"They live just next door."

The Vakaafis are gracious, just like their daughter. Mrs. Vakaafi goes to fetch me a fruit punch, obviously very at home here. She brings me back a coconut shell cup ornamented with hibiscus flowers and pours Dr. Neville some more rum, straight. Will takes a drink of his beer. I can see the bulge of his throat rise and fall out of the corner of my eye.

"You've come just in time, Angelie," says Dr. Neville. "We were about break into that glorious swine, weren't we?"

"As soon as Will's ready to start carving." It's Oliana, flushing like a red dahlia. She's come up carrying a tray of sliced mango, and her brother, Ku, is right behind her. He waves; a big bloke with a jolly laugh.

"The carving knives have been sharpened," she informs us. "Ku did a fine job."

"At your service," he says, winking at me. He leans in to my ear, scrunching up his nose.

"You smell like a posie," he says.

"I should smell like an evening in Paris."

Oliana gasps excitedly. "Evening in Paris! Rose gave me a bottle for my birthday, but Ku knocked it off my night stand and it shattered. I didn't mind losing the perfume so much, but I loved the bottle. Dark blue with a silver Eiffel Tower. The moon and the stars."

"You can have mine," I say.

Oliana gnaws on her lip. "I couldn't."

"No, really. I'll bring it by tomorrow."

Ku's smile just about splits his face in half. "I knew you were a good coconut."

I like Ku and tell him I missed him at the welcome last night. He's treated me like his favorite person on the island since I stepped off the boat, and that feels like the closest thing to home besides Mum and Aunt Kitty. He even offers me his elbow and walks me to the roasting pit, which Will doesn't seem to like one bit. The young master of the house gives me a look like *what are you doing that for?*

Dinner is not at all like the banquet for the good doctors Neville and Vogel. Niue is a close-knit place and people come over to eat any old time, so we don't even really sit down. We take pieces of pork as we want them and pick up mango off the platter. No plates or silverware, just napkins. The wood benches angled around the bonfire remain empty as we stand around stuffing our faces. I feel a bit stiff without Mum and Aunt Kitty around, but at least I've got Ku. He sticks with me the whole time, telling funny stories about how he and his friends scared a bunch of ladies at Matapa with their cliff-jumping.

"You should have seen the way their bums jiggled as they ran screaming out of the water," he tells me, demonstrating of course.

All the while, Will is stuck on pig-carving duty with his dad and shooting me daggers.

"Meet me at the plank," he whispers, placing a final slice of pork belly on my napkin. "You can slip away when my mum offers tea."

I bring Ku his food and watch him chew up the fatty bits like they're made of heaven. A little bell rings and I start, hoping it's Rose with a tea announcement. Pathetic, I know.

But it's not Rose.

It's Dr. Cornelius Kandinsky Neville all ready to tell his story. He's clearly a showman, and calls everyone around to come sit at the bonfire. Eyes open like an owl's, the flames reflected on his corneas, he looks a bit like the lusty demon from the Book of Tobit. Max Vogel sits behind him—haven't seen him all night. The German crosses his arms and regards the small crowd of us with an air of detachment. Don't like him one bit and I'm not at all sure I believe the whole "just a geologist" story everyone else on the island seems to have bought hook, line and sinker.

Standing off to the side, leaning against a pickling barrel, is Will Tongahai. There's pieces of crispy pig skin in his palm and he feeds them to a pair of fox terriers that have been running around the place all night. And there's a sweetness to the way he does it, I have to say. Pig skin or no pig skin, the dogs like him the best.

"Do you want to live forever?" Neville booms.

Most of us chuckle a bit. Will doesn't, I notice.

"Who hasn't beseeched a god with that request?" Neville takes a deep breath, his chest expanding. "Ah, but what if it was granted? And what if, as with every wish, it came along with a catch. There's always a catch. And forever isn't conferred upon just anyone. Not by a wise and just deity, anyway. If you are to receive the gift of immortality, then certainly more than a pound of flesh will be taken from you. Just ask Michael the Archangel, who was tasked with leading God's armies against Satan!"

"I have plenty of flesh to give," says Mr. Vakaafi, grabbing his middle.

Neville slaps his firm, flat belly and snickers. "If I could give you eternal life, Tane, I would."

"I'm sure you'd put your rum punch to good use on Niue for a hundred generations, at least." Rose raises her cup to a great roar all around.

"Wouldn't that be glorious?" Neville says. "To spend a life without end among generations of family and loved ones. Of course, that might be the ninth circle of hell for you, isn't that right Max?"

Max Vogel, with all the spirit of a slab of concrete, throws a macadamia nut in the air and catches it on his tongue. He tosses one to Neville, who clasps it in his hand and brings it to his lips, chewing and swallowing at leisure.

"No," Neville says. "I'm talking about rare souls who have been given an awesome fate. A burden of birth and death and love propelling their very essence through time—through the ravages of war and the long marches of survival. All for the love of each other, and the good of us. Dying of hunger and being born of disease. Burning at the stake for heresy and arriving again as the son of their very executioner. All the while having been given not merely life and eternal love, but a quest. A divine quandary that must be answered or else . . . or *else*."

He lets his S linger in a hiss, and a hush comes over us. Except for Ku, who keeps smacking his lips, wolfing down slices of pig. I watch Oliana give him a light kick on the shin.

"Or else what?" I say.

"Or else they may be thrust away from the great family of our earth and thrown into the lonely abyss of the universe. Or else all of humanity may suffer a devastation that could destroy it. Or else, in the ancient legends, is never a good thing, and it's rarely spelled out like a school assignment. Such beings as I speak of—Nin'ti was what the trinket seller in Egypt told my father they were called—Nin'ti are bound to unveil their quest the way someone like me is driven to unearth the past."

The islanders are spellbound, staring at Neville as if they expect him to turn into one of these creatures at any time. Not Will, though. His eyes are trained on the fire, absorbed in another world altogether it would seem.

"So," I say, and Will looks up. "These forever beings you're talking about have a quest, and they don't know what it is, but if they don't realize it, they'll be banished and we'll all become extinct or something?"

Neville leans his forearms on his thighs, the way he did on the boat when I watched him come in. He's got the same look on his face, too.

"Or something, yes."

"That's a crook deal," I say.

Neville smiles. "Eternity is very expensive."

"And what do these beings look like?" Will asks. "I mean, if they're one of us, just walking about. Can we identify them?"

Neville turns to Will.

"Their eyes, of course. As varied as their lives, as arcane as gems. As rich as the stratigraphic layers of the ground on which we live and die. If our eyes are the windows to our souls, theirs contain the very marrow from which a soul is created. A formidable substance indeed."

He turns from Will and his eyes bore into mine. I don't think anyone has ever looked at me quite the way Dr. Cornelius Kandinsky Neville is looking at me. As if I, myself, am a priceless object of ancient lore.

"Boo!" I say, and everyone just about leaps out of their skins. Will bursts out laughing and Neville claps his hands. Oliana snuggles into her brother's arms.

"Angelie!" she says. "You're going to give me nightmares."

I blow Oliana a kiss and she catches it, letting it loose on the top of her head with a bit of a twitter.

"Alright, alright," says Rose. "I think it's time for tea."

I DON'T KNOW why I listened to Will Tongahai when he told me to meet him at the plank, of all places. Should have ignored him for many reasons, but the most immediate one is that it's damned dark in the macadamia groves at night, even with a big old moon, and I can't bloody see well enough where I'm going. Emerging from the rows of trees, I do catch sight of the plank up ahead. A contorted branch of rock that juts off the plateau, it dangles over the sea, illuminated by unfettered moonlight and a heavy dusting of stars. It's a rather hypnotizing formation and I forget to even try to look where I'm stepping. For the damned second time I twist my ankle and but good.

"Damn," I say, bending down to give it a rub.

A shadow looms over me, long and lithesome, a black stain on a turf of dark indigo grasses.

"Your bones were broken and I was holding you."

Will's voice comes from behind me. Soft, like a sad melody. He's close enough that I can feel the heat of his body and I don't know how it is that I didn't hear him walking up.

"The sand was blowing all around us, lashing our faces, obscuring the sun and turning the day into night."

"Was that your dream?"

"Yes," he says.

Will puts his hand on my shoulder. His touch is like warm water and I shiver.

"My father says that around a full moon, dreams are made up of memories."

I look out at the man in the moon, suspended high above the water. "Aren't all dreams made up of memories in one way or another?"

"I suppose so," he whispers.

His finger trails up my neck inciting a legion of goose pimples and making my skin feel tender all over. I grab a fist full of grass to keep steady.

"Is that where your tattoos come from? Your dreams?"

His finger stops, resting gently at the base of my skull.

"Images of funeral pyres and night skies, like this one. Oceans of sand and flowers I've never seen before. Cities and people I don't know. They were all I dreamt about after I went away to school. Every time I closed my eyes."

He places his hands on my shoulders and my breath starts. I know he can hear it. Slowly, his fingers tiptoe under my collarbone, where he lets his palms rest. They're all hot and damp, like he ran all the way here to find me.

"There you are!"

It's Ku, and I just about fall over.

"Oliana's been looking for you, Will."

I stand up, bobbing on one foot like a jack-in-the-box.

"And you're here, too."

"I stumbled," I say, stupidly. "My ankle." As if that's an excuse to be out in the dark, alone with Will.

We all go quiet in one of those awkward silences.

"The moon will do that," Ku says, finally. "It's probably a good thing there won't be a full one at your *hifi ulu*, eh, Will?"

Will sticks his hands in his pockets and looks down. His braid overlays his backbone in the way of those spiny beasties in the outback.

"You're actually going to have one of those?" Part of me hates to think of Will cutting his long hair. It seems a part of him. But on Niue, hair-cutting ceremonies are crucial for a boy's journey to manhood. It makes a male child a man in the eyes of his Niue elders.

"Will was supposed to do it before he left for school, but he wouldn't," Ku tells me. "Told his parents a boy becomes a man when he takes on a man's responsibilities. Not when he cuts his hair." Ku slaps Will's arm. "That what you're going to do Will? Take on responsibilities? Maybe make an honest woman of my sister?"

My flesh runs absolutely cold and I look up at Will, my mouth gaping like an imbecile's.

"There's nothing dishonest about Oliana and me," Will says. "We were children."

"She cried her eyes out when your mum and dad shipped you off to England." Ku shrugs, crossing his arms over his chest. "And now, here you are."

"And here *I* go," I say, just about wanting to vomit. I test out my ankle and thank God it'll do. I'm not staying here another second.

"Wait," Ku says. "I'll walk you back in case you fall again."

He rushes up to me, but Will Tongahai doesn't follow. Damn him! Instead, he walks onto the plank and stands on its brink, his silhouette stamped onto the face of the very moon that's inked onto the back of his neck. His head is turned away from us and facing out towards the sea.

"*Ah'kwarah'a,*" I call out to him. The words just spill out of me and I cup my hands over my mouth, my heart batting away in my chest.

"What's that gobble-dee-goop?" Ku asks me.

Will cocks his head and I know he understands. Even if he can't possibly. Even if I've never known the words I spoke and can't imagine where they came from. I only know they were in my dream, and I wrote them down this morning as soon as I opened my eyes.

They mean, *I was born for you.*

Chapter 6

NEAR THE LEDGE at the drop off is where it's least dark, and Ku and I are determined to follow its line all the way back to my village. It really isn't that far, but a twisted ankle makes it bloody awful. I'm gimping along like a broken toy, and the only bright spot is that my pained expression looks to be about my actual physical pain, and not that Will Tongahai makes me do and say the strangest things. Or the fact that Will and Oliana had a thing going before he went off to school and that everyone on the island appears to fully expect that that thing will be a forever thing.

Don't know why I even care. He can go ahead and marry her if he wants. Not like I have any intention of remaining on this rock after the war or anything. I'd die of boredom a thousand times over.

"Go ahead," Ku says, crouching. "Hop on."

Ku's back, wide and muscular, ready for me, gleams in the night and I limp over to him. Climbing up, I wrap my arms around his neck and he stands with a kick-in-the-gut groan.

"You eat the whole pig, little A?"

"You're hardly one to talk," I say, smacking the top of his head.

I shouldn't be so shaken about damned Will, but I am.

I mean literally, I am shaking, and I have been since we left the plank. It was just a dream, after all. A dream that feels more real than anything I know, but it's still a damned dream. Ever since we got here, I've felt my old life slipping away from me, that's all. Even Dad and Jay being gone. Gone forever. That seems far away now. Not like it happened long ago—more like it happened to someone else. I haven't cried once about it since we arrived on Niue. Not even when I hear mum having a good blub like she always does nearly every day at the crack of dawn. When she wakes up and remembers that it's real. Her men are never coming back.

"I hope you're not in a crank," Ku says. "I mean, I was just teasing. And I've carried heavier sacks of coconut than you."

"What on earth are you talking about?"

"You're quiet, that's all," Ku says. "I haven't known you long, but I've never known you to be quiet."

I pinch his ear and bring my lips right up to it.

"You want another smack?" I ask him.

"From you? I'll take it."

Ku stops. Down below, I can hear the waves shattering at the base of the cliffs, and the sounds of a barn owl and a cuckoo in conversation.

"You tired?" I ask Ku. "I can walk, you know."

Although I'm not at all happy about that prospect.

"No, I'm fine," Ku says. "I was just . . . well, I was just wondering if maybe you're sore about what I said about Will. And my sister."

"Why would I be sore about that?" I try to be convincing on that one, really I do.

"Angelie, Will's a good bloke. He wouldn't set out to give you a hard time or anything. He's an odd bloke, though. Always has been."

"Yes," I say. "He is."

Ku puts me down and turns me towards him. Such a sweet face he's got. Handsome in the way of the good ones, with the kind of smile that's not lying to you, charming you into liking him more than he likes you. And just for the sport of it. He takes my hand and I let him. It's rough and tough-skinned from all the farm work he does, and patterned with cuts from cleaning fish. Some long-healed, some from yesterday. Can't see those scars now, but I have in the daylight, and I like them. These hard-working hands of his add to Ku's warmth and good-nature. A girl would be lucky to have a bloke like him weave his fingers through her own. Call her his sweetheart.

A girl who isn't me.

"You know," Ku says. "I can't blame Will for wanting to get to know you better, it's just that I . . ."

A sharp squealing noise cuts into whatever Ku was going to say next. It's come on the wind, from just where the Drs. Neville and Vogel were taking their geological samples this morning. Ku's brow scrunches up, but I know exactly what that sound is.

"Shhh," I say, giving a good listen. Yes, there it goes again.

The drop-off is still quite a ways off, up an incline leading off from the Tongahai's crop field. I limp towards it with Ku in tow, and he's whispering how it was probably just a bird.

"No bloody way," I tell him.

At the base of the incline, I look up and can barely make out the hunched forms of two figures. A red light blinks between them and I can catch gurgles of static above the draughts of wind that come up this time of night.

"Is it a radio?" Ku rasps.

"A radio transmitter," I tell him.

A series of taps and squealies toll over the drop-off, raining down on us in a light pitter of far-flung noise. I hear the unmistakable bark of German throughout it all.

"Is it those doctor blokes?" Ku asks.

"Who else?"

"Trying to pick up the news from the mainland, you think? Fat chance of that."

I shake my head.

"They're the ones doing the talking. Sending out some sort of message I think."

Ku takes a few strides up the incline and strains to have a look. "Why do you suppose they're doing that?"

A loose rock gets under foot and Ku wobbles, then skitters all the way back down to me, flailing those thick arms of his and calling out a big, long *waaaa* that can probably be heard on the other side of the fields, at Will's place.

"Dammit," I say.

Up top, the shadowy outlines of Drs. Neville and Vogel stand, Neville with his legs wide and his hands on his hips, and Vogel, all stiff. In fact, he barely looks human. More like a stake about to be pounded into the ground—or plunged into someone's heart.

"Who's there?"

I'm about to grab Ku and make a run for it when he starts waving his arms.

"Hello there," he says.

"That you, Ku?"

"O, yea," Ku says in that way of his that makes everyone want to be his friend. Kandi Neville, however, appears uncharmed.

"And who's that with you?"

I walk towards him a bit, trying my best at an even

gait. It's hard, what with my ankle and all. "Collecting soil samples again, are you, Dr. Neville?" I say.

The transmitter has been turned off, but I can still see the bare specter of its outline between them.

"It's late," Neville says, the whites of his eyes catching every possible glint of light.

"I was just taking Angelie here home," Ku tells him, being all helpful.

"But we're happy to stay to keep you fellows company," I say. "Your work is awfully fascinating."

Neville comes down from the drop-off, stepping into the shadows where Ku and I have been obscured from his view. I can see him better now. His customary good humor is all but gone, and I can smell the bitter tang of sweat infused in his shirt.

"We weren't trying to disturb you," Ku says. "We just heard something and wanted to know what it was."

"Can't blame us for being curious," I add.

Neville comes up close. Just a crumb closer than is polite. I can see the bulge of his ancient statue tucked into his shoulder holster, in the place where a gun would normally be. I think how odd it is that an archaeologist would have a pistol on Niue, and wonder where in the name of bloody St. Sebastian he put that pistol. I just hope Max Vogel doesn't have it trained on us.

Biting down hard on my lip, I watch Neville take in a deep breath through his nostrils. They flare wide, like his eyes, and make me want to turn and run right here and now. I don't though. No bloody way.

"Is there a difference, collecting samples at night or during the day?" I ask. "Geologically speaking, I mean?"

Max Vogel says something in German and I know he's talking about me because I hear him say "heiress," which means girl and I'm the only girl here. And it sure doesn't sound like he's saying anything particularly nice about me, but then again, nothing sounds nice in German, does it?

Neville answers him back and I have no idea what he says—didn't catch a word—but if I had to venture a guess, I'd say it was something along the lines of, "Keep your shirt on, mate, I'll handle this." I comfort myself with the thought that two missing persons on an island as tiny as Niue would cause a hubbub these two characters can't afford. Getting rid of our bodies, Ku's and mine, would prove pretty damned hard unless they took us way out to sea and dumped us there. Even if they threw us off this cliff, we'd just float right back in and wash up on shore. And that would wreck whatever it is they're doing for the Axis—yes, the Axis, I'm sure of it. They're in with the Germans and the Japanese and the Italians, out to stomp their bloody feet all over the world!

Neville lifts up his hand and puts his knuckle under my chin, tipping it up to meet his face. I take a breath just as deep as he did and flare up my nostrils. Two can play at this game.

"Go home, Angelie," he says softly. "A girl like you shouldn't be out at this time of night."

"A girl like me? You mean from Down Under?"

My voice cracks a bit, and Neville smiles. His teeth are so radiant under the moon, it's like they belong to a spirit.

"Something like that," he whispers. "Yes, something very much like that."

Chapter 7

HOW ABOUT *some time alone? It's not too much to ask for, I think.* I say this to Mum right before I take off for Avaiki cavern, and I'm not proud of myself or anything. Ancient statues, tattooed flesh, and a couple of suspicious buggers doing God knows what. That's two days, going on three, of living in a pulp novel is what's done it to me.

Of course, it's not lost on me that I'm going to a place that's been called the most mysterious and secluded spot on the island. Guess I'm just begging for trouble. Or excitement, as *he who shall not be named* seems to think.

I walk the sea track down a steep line of stairs, not at all upset about missing supper. My ankle's pretty good today, but it's still a bit tricky here, what with rope hand-holds and my not wearing exactly the best shoes in the world for such a venture. They're an old pair of peep-toe sandals that hardly grip the slippery rocks at all, but at least I don't mind if they get ruined.

All this for just a bit of beauty, not that it's scarce on Savage Island. Plus a couple of hours without Aunt Kitty's warnings about everything but the real dangers here.

"Don't be silly, Angelie," Kitty said at breakfast. "That Neville bloke's delightful. And God only knows all the things archaeologists do, oh my word. I'm sure they were just doing that."

"What?" I said. "Name it!"

"The things they do!" She slammed a flyswatter down, murdering a checkered beetle who wasn't doing anything to harm anyone. "Darned bugs are going to kill us!"

After that, she just brushed me off about what Ku and I saw last night. Nice.

And then there's Will. Dammit! I swore I wasn't going to say his name—not even to myself. Or think about him for that matter! And I'm not! From here on out. Not about his storied skin, or the way he devoured me in a kiss after the banquet for those Axis snoops. Or the fact that he did a lot more than that in a dream I had early this morning, just before I pretty much screamed myself awake. Mum thought I was having a nightmare.

I almost wish.

It was a dream of wild colors and a chilly night. Skin against skin. Whispers in that language, cooing softly in my ear. *I live and die with you, Sherin.*

Sherin. Sounds like the word for a fine cloth. Maybe a wrap a rich lady would wear to the opera.

I take a deep, deep breath and it does feel good to be alone. For all of its remoteness and sparse population, Niue is not a place for solitude. Someone is always somewhere—asking for help, or if they can help you, joining along as you try to have a stroll, inviting you for supper and breakfast and tea. Not that it isn't lovely, but I do get tired of always being in the company of others. That's why supper is just the perfect time to get away, since most islanders are either making food or eating it. Plus, it's low tide, which I've been told is really the only safe time to visit Avaiki. Otherwise it can flood completely and become an impassable wreck.

The path I'm trudging along brings me to a modest gap

in the limestone cliffs. It's basically a human-sized mouse hole ringed with a garland of curly vines, and looks just the way Ku described. I step into a cave of sepia and shadows, following a light that promises sun. Edging around all sorts of rock formations, from twisted spines that come up from the ground to simple boulders, smoothed from violent rushes of ocean tides, I make my way without much trouble. Finally, I veer to the right through an opening that doesn't look like much.

"No bloody way," I say.

I stop dead in my tracks. The sea path has brought me to the most extraordinary place. I've come up on a ledge into a grotto that is literally the size of a cathedral. There's a tall complex of white stalactites that go from the ceiling almost all the way down into a pool of water that is as close to the color of my eyes as anything I've ever seen. Some of the stalactites have the appearance of fossilized bones, like ones of a primeval ogre. Others drip down the cave wall like melted wax. There are tinier caves all over this chamber, making it look like honeycomb. Many of the rocks are covered with moss, and those that aren't appear brushed with cobalt blue, and vivid pink and orange streaks befitting an abstract painting.

The cave is sheltering, but opens out onto the Pacific like the mouth of a god. Late afternoon sun streams in, as if inviting me to stay. And in the most peculiar way, I feel as if I'm visiting an old friend.

Climbing my way down to the pool, I find it's not too hard a trek. The water is quite low this time of day, probably up to my neck by the looks of it. I know during storm surges it can rise all the way up to the ledge where I came in, some four or five yards above, flooding some of the smaller chambers.

I scale a knurled hunk of coral that looks out over the pool, watching a few tiny fish dart to and fro in a brilliant red group. Here, I unbutton my dress, stripping down to my slip. Feels sublime to stand by my lonesome in a place so old, made entirely by the hands of nature. A part of the supercontinent, maybe. Taking a deep breath, I let my body go slack and simply fall into the water. Cool, fresh, surprising. I feel as if I've been baptized. For a few holy minutes I float on my back with eyes closed, the calm waters lapping gently against my face.

And when I open them, I see the sunlight speckling the ceiling high above me. A white tern has found its way into the cave, gliding in a circle. It lands on the ledge where I came in, next to a pair of sun-browned feet.

"Gadzooks," I gasp.

I kick my feet, plunging them down into the water and flutter my arms about. The water's a bit deeper than I thought, and I can't touch my toes to the bottom, so I have to tread water.

"You found Avaiki," Will says.

He's standing there in an undershirt and a pair of cotton trousers cut off at the knees. His hair is loose and flowing all the way to his hips. I guess he was thinking of going for a swim, too. In a strong and graceful arc, Will dives from the ledge, cracking the surface of the water like a bolt of lightning. He swims right under me and surfaces with a smile, backstroking around the pool for a bit.

"You know, the ancient kings used to bathe here," he tells me. "They did so alone, as they were the only ones considered worthy of entering the cavern."

"I can see why," I say. "It's the most beautiful place I've ever been."

Will makes his way to me, pulling himself along the

crust of the cave wall. He comes up close, his hair drifting about him like tentacles.

"I come here to get away from everyone," he says. "And I never tire of it."

He reaches out, touching my bottom lip with his index finger, and I don't quite know what to do.

"You're turning blue," he says. "We better get out of the water for a while."

I follow Will around to a hunk of coral reef with lots of ridges. He goes out first and then helps me up. Here I am, dripping wet, with my slip sticking to me like wallpaper. I wrap my arms over my breasts and Will is good enough to keep his eyes trained on my face. I'm not as disciplined, I'm afraid. It's hard not to notice the bright hues of his tattooed skin through the thin, soaked cotton of his undershirt.

"Sorry," I say.

"I don't mind."

Will steps closer and I'm afraid he might try and kiss me again. Even more afraid that I want him to.

"Would you like to see," he says.

I look around, although I'm sure we're alone. Nodding, I swallow much too loudly.

Will's eyes, even more beautiful than this cave, with their rivers of amber and blood, lock onto mine. He crisscrosses his arms over his chest and grips the bottom of his shirt, peeling it off like a layer of skin. But he doesn't stop there. Next, he unties the waist of his trousers and pulls those off, too, kicking them off to the side. He stands there before me without a stitch on, and a queer chirp escapes my lips. My knees nearly buckle and I look away, crushing my palms over my face.

"Go ahead and look," he says. "You should start at my feet. It's what I saw in my dream on my first night in Canterbury."

I want to see him more than anything, but I just don't know if I have it in me to take my hands away and pry open my eyes. My shoulders start to shake and I can't stop the tears now. Of longing and grief and God knows what else? I stand there and sob in front of a stark naked Will Tongahai like I'm some sort of idiot.

"It's okay," he says. "I cried, too. Each time I went back to the inkmaster. He thought it was because I didn't like needles, I think."

He laughs a little and I guess that breaks the ice a bit, but I'm still a mess.

Will reaches out and touches my hair, lightly pinching a lock of it and riding his fingers down to where it ends, just below my shoulders.

"It was the hands I found so compelling," he says, referring to the delicate images on his feet. The ones I'd caught a glimpse of when we ate lunch at the drop-off the other day.

"Angelie," he says. "You don't have to look at anything you don't want to."

I stop gasping and give a good hiccup. The tears haven't quit flowing, but I've got a grip on myself at least. Taking a good lungful, I wipe my nose with the bottom of my slip and rub my eyes. I lick my lips, tucking my hair behind my ear and finally dare to glance down at his feet. That refined pair of hands, their skin the pinkish brown of the Niue—almost—rest on his ankle, its fingers opening up to his calves. They're determined hands set to do some work, like Aunt Kitty's when she's about to make a garment. They hold a flower the likes of which I've never seen, an explosion of deep indigo and yellow with petals like torn flesh. Up further are more exotic cuttings, ones with green and pinkish orange leaves in the shape of feathers and some fiery pistols pointed like thorns.

My gaze travels up his leg—I can't help it. A garden of wild and alien flora grows in a tangle up from his knee to the base of his hip. There, I see the faces of some flowers I do recognize—orchids. They bloom over a backdrop that's faint and the color of sepia, like an old photograph. I think it's of the Citadel in Cairo, but it's hard to say since I've only seen that in books. Will doesn't bother covering up, and somehow that's fine now. Not at all a scandal. In fact, I find I'm not crying anymore.

I tip my head to view his hips. On the flower side is the face of an infant. A boy, I think. I reach out and stroke his cheek as if he were mine. A swell of love and longing makes my heart feel as if it will up and float away like a balloon. On the other side is a circular pattern of flying glass, blown from a cathedral's window during an act of war or maybe from the angry winds of a raging storm. The pieces disappear into the interior of his thigh, becoming tiny fish, silver and blue. That leg is patterned with what look like medieval Celtic images of knots and dragons and crosses. Somehow it all fits together.

On Will's torso is a dazzling sunset, upside down, it would appear. It shines its dying light onto a series of beguiling images. There are birds in the oriental style, a Byzantine portrait of a man, all gold and winter colors. A gorgeous string of hieroglyphs that look like notes of music. Some of the images are of fighting, like tiny men in a battle. Others appear loving, all twisted together as if in some sort of embrace. A crossed set of swords lies just under his collarbone, as if lifting his head to the heavens.

All of it magnificent. So fine. As if conceived by a genius and painted by a master.

I walk around to his back, breathless. Will lifts up his hair and I see the blue blood moon at the nape of his neck.

It pours down on a night sky above a desert landscape that speaks of eternity, and is overlaid by two determined arrows painted along his spine. Then, of course, are the flames. All over his arm, as if they might, at any time, spread and consume him. Consume us both.

I lift my hand to touch him there, sure that he'll be too hot to the touch. But he's not. In fact, his skin is still cool from our swim. I watch the goose pimples spread as the pads of my fingertips move up his bicep and over to his shoulder blades. Angel's wings for sure. There, looking over the top of his shoulder is the face of a young woman; the one wrapped around the length of his other arm. It's heart-shaped, her face, and she's got heavy brows and full lips. Nothing like me at all. But there are her eyes. Shaped like almonds and exactly the color of mine.

Will starts to tremble.

"Come to me," he whispers.

And I do.

Chapter 8

MY EYES ARE SO HEAVY it takes real effort to lift my
eyelids. The light has changed. A warmer color, more
like mustard than lemon. I'm lying on my arm and have lost
all feeling in my fingers. I wonder how long I've been asleep.
Beneath my head, I can hear Will's heartbeat. Feel it, too.
His skin is soft and damp. Will's fingers are stroking ever so
gently along my spine. He wishes me awake, I think.

I feel I should say something. One of us should. But I
don't dare speak. It's not that I regret what we did. I don't.
Not at all. And not just because it felt so good. Here, in
the cave, it's like we know everything about the other. As
if we've done this a thousand times before, even if it feels
like the first.

The moss is soft as fur—a thick carpet on a prickly rock. I
dig my fingers into it as if I'm scratching a dog, and run my
lips along a stream of sunlight inked up from Will's belly. I
kiss his nipple. Maybe we don't need words. Not yet.

I GAZE AT OUR BODIES, mine all fresh cream and Will's an
explosion of color, like the skin of a tropical snake. He runs
his hands all over me and I wish he'd never stop.

"The sun's going down," he whispers. "We'll have to swim out of here."

I wish we never had to leave

"I didn't know we could swim out."

"You can if you know what you're doing."

Will rolls off of me part way and rests his head on his elbow, looking at me. The pleased smile on his face is a bit candid, but I suspect I'm wearing one a lot like it, too. Now I feel awfully shy.

"Don't look away," he says. "I love your face."

His fingers tiptoe over my shoulder.

"What is it?" I say, although I'm not sure I want to know.

His smile turns to mischief and I can feel my cheeks burning red.

"You better say whatever it is you want to say," I tell him.

Will sits up a little further, his eyes travelling down my body.

"You seemed to like it."

It's not just my cheeks that are burning now.

"Yes," I say. "You did, too. Is that such a surprise?"

Will wrinkles his brow some and lifts up the corner of his mouth. "Well, I mean. Not every girl likes it the first time around."

I rise up, leaning back onto my elbows, and stretch a bit.

"Not every girl likes it in your vast experience of deflowering young maidens?"

Will kisses the top of my breast so sweetly and rests his chin just beneath my collar.

"Not vast experience, no."

"So all the English girls in Canterbury were easy prey for you, is that it? With your long hair and island ways?"

"Just one other girl, Angelie," he says, and it feels like a hard stab from an ice pick.

"Do you keep in touch with this fancy girl from your *oh, so English* boarding school?"

Will goes silent, and I feel a terrible dread. He takes a deep breath and lies on his back.

"She wasn't English," he finally says.

And now I feel terribly naked all of a sudden. Like Eve. I want to crawl over and get my clothes—dress before another word is spoken.

"Scottish, maybe?" I say.

Nothing. Not a sound.

"Don't tell me what I think you're going to tell me. For God's sake, don't say it was Oliana."

"We were kids. I made that clear."

"Kids don't do this! Ku asked if you were going to make an honest woman of Oliana and you said there was nothing to make honest."

"No, I said there was nothing dishonest between us and there isn't."

"Not to you, but what about her and me!"

I feel ridiculous standing up wearing only what God gave me, but there's little else I can do. My slip is dank and cold as a foggy night, but I pull it over my head anyway.

"Angelie, don't," Will says. He gets up, too, and comes over to me, ignoring his clothes, or lack thereof, entirely.

"What do you mean, don't? Oliana is my friend, sort of, and you made it seem like some childhood crush between you—not a love affair!"

"It *was* a childhood crush," Will tells me. "It's just. Well, things are different here, that's all. We don't look at things quite the way you do."

I step into my dress and try to button it, but my hands are shaking so much that I simply can't manage.

"Well, it doesn't look all that different when I see the way she looks at you, and don't tell me you haven't noticed," I say. "Dammit, Will, this is supposed to mean something!"

"It does!"

"Until when – someone else comes along? And then you'll describe me as what? A crush on a girl from the mainland? A bit of excitement after getting dragged back here from London—oh, excuse me, *Canterbury*."

Will swats my trembling hands away and begins buttoning me up. I don't know why I let him, but I do.

"I'm not the one looking for excitement," he says, teeth all clenched like all of this is my fault! "You've made it perfectly clear it's dull around here for your tastes."

"Really?" I say. "Is that why you tried to join the Navy? Because you hate excitement so much?"

"No!"

Will runs his fingers through his hair part way and it's a marvel they don't get tangled up. Damn his hair is lovely. It's taking everything I've got not to burst into tears and I'm not doing that! I bite my lip to keep it from quivering and force myself not to cast my eyes away like a coward. He seems sad and confused and I don't like it at all that I'm starting to feel sympathy for him.

"I didn't go to join the war because I was bored," Will finally says. He looks me straight in the eye. "I didn't want to. I felt I had to. I knew I'd be good at it."

Will walks over and lifts his cut-up pants off the edge of our moss rock. He puts them on slowly, gazing down into the water. "You're right that I didn't want to come back here," he says. "I guess I could have run off again, defied my parents, but that didn't feel right either. And not just because I'm all they've got and my dad needs me to be here for my mum in case something happens to him. To be honest, I didn't know why I came back, until I saw you."

Somehow the word "Oh" escapes my lips and that seems a pathetic thing to say. Especially since I don't even know what he means by that and I have no intention of asking.

"Is that such a terrible thing, Angelie?" Will says, just above a whisper. "When I first saw you that night when those men came—Dr. Neville and Dr. Vogel. It was like an answer. Maybe to a prayer, or a question I didn't know I was asking. I thought maybe you felt it, too."

Oh, God, I do want to kiss him. Not just those arrogant lips of his, but all over. Every inch of his painted up flesh. I want to slap that handsome face and tear at his hair. Most of all, I want to stay.

"Damn you, Will Tongahai!"

I jump, fully clothed mind you, into the cool, green pool and swim out to the mouth of the cave. Will is behind me, shouting something about hot-orange coral. I hear him jump in and I start to swim faster. The coral reef is coming up closer as I get into the shallower parts that lead to the beach. I kick harder and feel a sting above my ankle, strangely warm, and I wonder if I didn't catch a bite from one of the sea snakes.

"Stop!" Will calls out. "Stop right there!"

I want to call back and tell him to mind his own business. Maybe Oliana listens to whatever he tells her, but I'm under no obligation to do so, thank you very much.

"Dammit, Angelie, you're going to slice yourself to bits!"

I start to tell him to keep his advice to himself, but I'm feeling lightheaded all of a sudden. Like when you get up from bed much too fast and those blinking lights appear before your eyes. And I'm a bit nauseous, too. Will is swimming towards me and I'm sure I have him to blame for all of this. For the way he makes me feel. And not only me, apparently. Oliana. She's felt his touch like I did this afternoon. Maybe he kissed her just as he did me . . . deep kisses at my mouth, and tender ones, featherlike, all over. I can't help it, I start to relive our afternoon over again. The way he looked at me as my wet slip dropped in a heap at my feet. The way he laid me down. Makes me feel heavy. My head falls under the water and I watch a bubble escape my lips.

The water is cool and so soft to touch. Like Will. I think I could float here forever, never taking another breath.

"Breathe, Angelie, for God's sake!"

Above water again, strong arms about me. I open my eyes a little and there he is. Will's more than handsome face. My lungs contract and I cough up some harsh, salty water. Burns my throat.

"There you go. Just float. Don't move, alright?"

He's pulling me along, my arms and legs going numb. I watch the hot-orange coral under the water as it recedes from us and notice how the early evening sun is just the same color. How lovely. A bright ribbon of crimson follows us, just like the cloudy trail of smoke from the back of an airplane. It rather mesmerizes me.

"Look, Will," I say, and he shushes me gently, kissing the top of my head.

Just to the side of us is a shadow, a thin oval moving about. Very graceful. Like Will. The way he dove into the pool at Avaiki and cut through the water beneath my feet before coming up next to me. The shadow comes close, too, and I try to reach out to it, but Will grabs my hand and turns me in the water just before we're bumped, and hard. Something rough as rock scrapes by my leg, and a full rush of adrenaline wakes me from my dreamy stupor.

"Hold onto me!"

I try to wrap my arms around Will's neck, but it's not

easy. My hands are tingling and not quite right. All the while, Will is making powerful strokes, and we're moving faster through the water. The red ribbon continues to follow us, and it's then that I notice just what that ribbon is. Blood! A lot of it. And it's coming from me!

"Oh, God!" I scream.

My arms flap up and I let go of Will, dropping right under the water again as if I've forgotten how to swim. He pulls me up.

"Don't panic," he says. "It'll be alright. We're going to have to get to the beach through the coral. It's razor sharp, so stay on top of me and I'll try to make sure you don't get cut again."

I'm about to ask him why in hell's bells we have to go through razor sharp coral to get to the beach, when it becomes abundantly clear. The shadow, and clearly the thing that rammed into us, is streaming towards us once again, only this time it's obvious what it is. It's a shark, and a pretty big shark at that. At least the size of Will. And I know he said not to panic, but I can't help it. I don't flail and scream like I did before, but I go stone cold with terror and can't move at all. Will sees what's going on and puts his arm around me tight, holding me to him like we're one. His other arm is free and I can feel his legs kicking to keep us above water.

The shark has circled us a couple of times, coming really close, and it looks like he's set to do it again. As he swims up, I can actually see the unholy bugger's eyes, as dead and black as they are in pictures. And I don't think the horrible beast is just going to make a pass this time, like he did the last. He means business.

But apparently, so does Will. I was so consumed by the damned shark that I'd almost forgotten about Will. It's hard to think clearly when you're about to become dinner for a hungry ocean monster! A real, actual danger for swimmers on the island of Niue. Particularly ones bleeding out into the shallows at rising tide.

Will, however, is not as fatalistic as I am and thank God! As the creature comes up, his arm rises out of the water, fist clenched in the air, and bears down onto the shark's nose! The creature flips its tail and swims away like a chastised dog, and Will starts swimming fast again towards the coral.

"We need to hurry," he says. "It'll be back, and might bring friends."

In no more than a minute, I start to see the coral coming up beneath us again. Will rolls me on top of him and swims on his back; the damned coral looks like it's right there underneath us, just inches away. I put my cheek on Will's chest and pinch my eyes shut.

"It's alright," he says. "He won't follow us here."

We slow quite a bit as Will tries to navigate the coral without getting all cut up. His breath is coming in huffs and he bites down on his lip.

"I can swim on my own," I say, but I can't right now and I know it. My limbs are like noodles and I'm sure I just keep bleeding and bleeding, but I don't want to look. Finally, Will stops. He scoops his arms under me and hunkers down in the water, right on the coral. It's that shallow now.

"I'll have to walk it the rest of the way," he says.

He holds me close to his chest and stands up. We're not that far from the beach, thank God, but right at the edge of the hot orange coral, which goes on for another few yards, until it fades into the plain, rough rock at the shoreline. Will starts walking, quick and sure, not too careful as to hesitate. It almost feels like we're flying above the water.

And when we make it to the beach, he doesn't set me down, but keeps walking. All the way back up the path and into the raffish snarl of trees and bushes, until we make it to the first house we see. A thatched house with a yard and garden; a stack of coconuts piled up like cannonballs on a picnic bench out front.

My adrenaline no longer pumping, I'm feeling weaker by the second. Strange and otherworldly, like I did when I sank under the water. I can hear Will calling out for help, and the last thing I see as we approach the thatched little house is its front door opening, and Oliana standing there with her mouth open wide as an ostrich egg.

Chapter 9

WILL'S BACK is painted red with blood. In the dim light of the Vakaafi's home it's difficult to tell how many cuts he got swimming over the reef as he brought me to shore. I want to reach out to him, kiss his wounds all over, but there's someone else here with us.

"What were you doing out there?" Oliana says, glancing back at me.

Will ignores her question and comes over to the bamboo sofa where I'm laid out.

"She's terribly pale," Oliana whispers.

"I think she's lost a lot of blood," he tells her.

I do hate being talked about like I'm not even here, and by Oliana of all people. But I'm too weak to join in and speak up for myself. All I can do is watch and listen and breathe. And imagine all sorts of things as I look at the two of them standing there together. It's a good thing I'm too damned wrecked to cry.

Will checks the bandage he put on my leg, wincing at how the blood is soaking through. He takes two hard-won steps towards the window and peers out. He's limping something awful and I look down to find he's leaving a gruesome trail of bloody footprints in his wake. He must have cut the dickens out of his feet, too.

"They'll be back soon," Oliana reassures him. "And with

the *taulaatua*. In the meantime, you need to sit down and let me clean you up."

"An herbalist isn't going to help her!"

Oliana's lip is trembling and she looks *this close* to bursting out into one howl of a sob. The kind you can't stop once it starts, no matter what you do. And I know it's not just because Will's a bloody mess. It's because she knows he became a bloody mess for the likes of me.

"You look frightful, you know," she murmurs. "Please."

Will shakes his head. "I'm fine."

The door swings open, bringing with it a gust of ocean wind that gives me prickly goosebumps. Who is it but Drs. Neville and Vogel, the Batman and Robin of some hellish underworld.

"We ran into your father as he was heading to the healers place," that Dr. Neville says to Oliana. "Thought we might get here sooner." He looks down at me and takes a big, deep breath. I guess I look that good. "Got any more clean linens?"

Will turns to Oliana and I hear Neville say, "Holy Zeus and Hera," as he gets a look at Will's back.

"And by more clean linens, I mean a lot more," Neville clarifies.

"It's not as bad as it appears," Will says.

"Well," Neville tells him. "I'll be the judge of that."

If I could summon the energy for a single sentence I'd ask him how he seems to think he knows so much about the medical arts, when he supposedly deals in old, dead things buried deep in the ground. And why Max Vogel defers to him like he's some sort of African god.

"Your good buddy Hitler would have no use for you," I hear myself mumble. "He'd throw you right in a cell with Jesse Owens if he could."

"Is that so?" Neville says.

Then it's like the whole rooms gets all wobbly on me. Fuzzy at the edges. The last thing I see is Will's face, full of worry, leaning in to mine. I think he caresses my hair just as everything starts to dim.

I WAKE UP GROGGY, but different. Like I've been filled in, and am not just some phantom anymore. Turned on my side, I face the flowery cushions of the Vakaafi's sofa. A hand is stroking my head, but it's not Will's, it's my mum's.

"She'll be alright."

That's the medicine lady talking—about me, I presume. I recognize her voice, all husky and raw, like she's been chattering all day.

"But you need to drink your juice, or you won't be in much better shape than that girl of yours."

"She's been out for so long," my mum says, tracing a finger around the curve of my ear.

I move my arm a bit, and learn quite fast that it was a bad idea. My arm's got a big needle in it. One that's taped down, and with a long red spaghetti noodle of a plastic tube coming out of it. That tube's connected to a glass bottle filled with blood, and I almost want to pass out again just looking at it.

"She's awake."

Now that's Will's voice. I hear him slog over and crouch down next to my mum as I try to turn onto my back oh so carefully.

"Angelie don't," my mum starts. Will puts his hands on my back and rolls me over so I don't pull on the blood drip that's attached to my aching arm. As I bend my leg, a sharp pain takes hold of my calf, making me jerk up. Will braces my shoulders before I can send the whole glass bottle of blood crashing to the floor.

His face remains wrought with concern, so I guess I'm still not looking my best. I give him the once over, too, and notice his feet are all bandaged up. He's standing on them, so they can't be so bad, but he doesn't seem comfortable by any stretch. He's got a shirt on, and it's long-sleeved, covering pretty much all of his cuts, not to mention his tattoos. And he's changed into pants.

"How are you feeling?" he asks me.

"I should ask you the same."

"I'm not the one who nearly died. Dr. Neville feared you might lose part of your leg."

Dr. Neville. "What would he know?" I say.

I hear my mum draw in a breath and remember all at once that she's here, too. I turn towards her as she leans over, bending down and leaving kisses on my forehead. She's teared up and must be thinking about Dad and Jay. How I had one foot into whatever heavenly pub they're nursing their coldies in.

"Will," she says. "He saved your life."

"It's you who did that," Will says. "You and our distinguished guests."

My mum sits up and takes his face in her hands. Poor thing has mascara running all the way down her face.

"I gave her a bit of blood, but if you hadn't brought her here so quickly—and with those gashes all over your feet—she'd be a gonner."

Will goes to open his mouth, but Oliana pipes up from across the room. Her voice is trembling with anger and it sounds like she might just flip her wig.

"Don't you dare brush this off, Will Tongahai," Oliana says. "You got near on a hundred stitches total."

"Flesh wounds, Oliana. Not any major vessels," he tells her, and it sounds like this rhubarb's been going on for a while between them.

I get up the courage to let my eyes fall on Oliana, but she's beat me to it, giving me a stink eye to end all stink eyes. I suppose I can't blame her. Behind her, on her mother's bureau is the bottle of Evening in Paris I dropped by. She sees my eyes flit to it and turns her head sharp and quick.

"Thank you for helping me," I say, and she shrugs.

There's a tentative knock at the door and Oliana goes to answer it, keeping her arms crossed over her breasts until she actually has to unlock them to open up. It's Max Vogel, and he comes in whispering in that mean accent of his, asking if I'm awake and how I'm doing and all that. It's the most I've heard him say in one go. He marches over and comes right at me, taking my head in his hands like a vice and lifting up my eyelids with his big German thumbs.

"My eyes turned to rocks, Herr Geologist? People do tell me they're as green as emeralds."

He slants toward me, close enough that I can smell his schnitzel breath. We're eye to eye now, and his are as grey as a thunder cloud.

"She's sounding more like herself," he says with a bit of a snicker.

But at least it makes mum laugh. Even Will breaks a smile. Not Oliana, who's back to standing with her arms crossed up and not at all willing to be amused by anything that has to do with me.

Vogel digs into the leather sack he's got tied at his waist and pulls out two pill bottles, handing one to my mum and the other to Will.

"Anti-biotics," he says. "Three times a day."

"Where'd you get those?" I mumble.

I can't imagine Niue has much of a supply, unless our trusty *taulaatua* managed to barter with the barge captain last time he came.

Vogel pretends like he didn't hear me and sits at the edge of the sofa, starting to unravel the mottled linen around my leg. As he lifts up the very last layer, all sticky with brown blood, I'm treated to a plum view of a straight, long scar that's been mended by God only knows how many stitches. Next to it is a rough, raw patch of skin that must be where the shark grazed me. I can't help letting go of a horrorstruck "ugh."

"Doesn't look so bad," Will says, giving me a sweet grin that makes my stomach go all sideways.

"It's dreadful," Oliana says. "Poor girl will never want to wear a dress again."

Will gives her a look.

"Who cares about dresses," my mum says. "As long as you're alright."

"The scar will fade," Vogel chimes in.

"From your vast knowledge of scars?" I ask him.

Vogel looks as if he's about to say something, but then stops. He takes his time re-wrapping my leg good and tight while the whole rooms stays silent as a church. My fault, I guess. When he's finished, he stands up and squares his shoulders, considering me for what feels like a plenty long time. I wish he'd just go. But he doesn't. Instead, he begins unbuttoning his shirt. No one knows quite what to say about it, and even Oliana shoots me a look, wondering what the kraut is up to. As he pulls his shirt out of his pants and peels it off his torso, he exposes a lean and hairless chest. Strangely muscled like he's used to lifting heavy things. He smirks a bit when he turns around, revealing a back that is literally covered with raised, mostly white scars, with a few pink ones where the thickest parts of his flesh was mauled. Truly, there's not a portion of his back that hasn't been mutilated by the lash of a whip, the burn of an iron, a straight razor. It's hard to even say all of the ways he's been abused.

"Dear God," my mum gasps.

I hear Will's sharp intake of breath and Oliana's whimper. Vogel is as stiff and steady as the trunk of a tree.

"Who did that to you?" I ask him.

The German bends down, picking his shirt up off the floor. He puts it back on, leaving the front unbuttoned.

"My brother," he says.

Nodding at mum, then the rest of us, he walks straight out the door, which seems to close all by itself like when Dracula leaves a room.

With a brother like that, it's no wonder he became a Nazi.

Chapter 10

NEVER OCCURRED to me that recovering from a damned cut—a big cut, mind you, but still a cut—would have me hobbling along on a pair of ancient crutches with the underarm pads nearly worn to the wood.

"Stupid buggers!" Didn't mean to say that out loud, and Ku sneaks me a look, trying not to laugh. We're coming away from the *taulaatua*, Ku and I, where the gash on my leg was soaked in fusty-smelling herbs by our resident witch-doctress, who, unlike Oliana, seems to think I will be back in skirts one day. Said witch-doctress is the only person on this rock who doesn't feel I have to lay in bed all day moaning, either. We're becoming quite good friends, actually.

"Bollocks!" I can't seem to stop cursing, but these glorified sticks really hurt, digging in at the bone and giving me the start of nasty purple bruises. I stop, plucking them out from underneath my arms, and leaning them on the tall, tin fence that surrounds the back of the fish market.

"Come on, Angelie, Dr. Neville says you should keep weight off your leg for at least three days."

"Dr. Neville is an archeologist, Ku, not a surgeon for Pete's sake."

Ku shakes his head.

"He sure seems to know plenty about doctoring. Filled you up with all new blood after you lost so much of your own."

"Hmm," I say, favoring my left leg and dragging these damned sticks down the street. It's an oddly overcast day, making even the trees look gray, and I wonder if it isn't contributing to my already peevish mood. I realize this is the first day since we arrived on Niue that hasn't been simply glorious.

"Angelie!"

Neville himself. Here he comes waving at me like a long-lost friend. At least Vogel's not with him.

"Dr. Neville," I say.

Ku gives him a big "hiya!"

"It's good to see you looking well," Neville tells me. "Certainly well enough to forgo your crutches, I see."

I shrug a bit and Ku starts to snicker again, so I give him a good pinch in the arm, nails and all.

"Ouch, you viper!"

I bat my eyes all innocent at him.

"Have you seen your friend Will?" Neville asks, and my heart just about drops out of me like a bomb.

"No," I say. It's technically true. He's come by the house a few times, but I made Mum send him away. I just can't. Not yet. I need to sort out how I feel about what went on between him and Oliana, not to mention the fact that I've hardly even gotten over the fact that I'm not a virgin anymore. Aunt Kitty would about die if she knew I hadn't saved myself for my wedding night. I guess I always thought I would, too. But that Will. Ugh, that Will!

"If you do see him, could you ask him to come by our cabin?"

"I won't. See him, I mean."

Dr. Neville gives me one of those looks that full-on adults give younger adults when they're feeling a certain combination of pity and amusement.

"If, by chance, I do see him, shall I tell him what it's about?"

Neville gives up a smile, but one that feels about as armored as a chain-link fence wrapped in barbed wire.

"He'll know."

Dr. Neville pats my shoulder. He shakes Ku's hand before moving past us and on down the street. His normally graceful walk all full of clipped urgency.

BY THE TIME WE ARRIVE at my place, my leg feels like it's been stuffed with bolts of lightning. I take the crutches from Ku and use them for the last few steps to the front door, if for no other reason than Mum would just about have a fit if she knew I was going against doctor's orders. Ever since the shark incident, as it's now called, she's not only come to worship Will, but Neville and Vogel, too, even though I've told her they're up to no good.

"You want me to put on some tea?" I ask Ku just as I'm about to open the front door. And he's about to answer when I hear voices coming from inside. I put my finger to my lips and squeeze his forearm.

"She's been gone for hours," Mum says. "She should be resting, but she cooks up any excuse to get out of here. I've got a good mind to tie her to the bed while she's napping and see what she does with that."

"But you're sure she went to the *taulaatua*?"

It's Will!

"I'm not sure of anything anymore when it comes to her," Mum tells him.

"Psst." Ku tugs on my sleeve. "We going to stand out here all day?"

I shush Ku, but at least he's bothering to whisper.

"Angelie, what's your problem?"

"Come on," I say, gritting my teeth and starting to hobble away as quietly as my creaky crutches will allow. Ku follows, kicking some dried, fallen palm branches out of our way.

"You can't avoid him forever, you know."

I roll my eyes pretty much all the way to the heavens and pick up my pace.

"I just don't want to see him today, okay? And what's it to you?"

Ku's face goes all wounded and I properly hate myself now. I stop to give him the whole of my attention. A good friend like him deserves that.

"I'm sorry."

Ku takes a deep breath that makes his chest puff up like a marshmallow. "It's obvious, you know."

"What?"

Ku gives me that look of his. The one that should melt my heart.

"You and Will. The way he looks at you. The way you can hardly stand looking at him."

"Don't be ridiculous."

All this talk of this look and that look makes me right want to dive off the plateau and swim back to Sydney.

"Oh, no?" Ku says, one thin, elegant eyebrow raised up like an inchworm. "Then why are you running away from him right now?"

I narrow my eyes at Ku and lean on one of my crutches, almost wishing I had lost my leg since the damned thing hurts so much.

"Shouldn't you be trying to throw your sister at Will Tongahai, instead of some mad mainlander girl?"

Ku's staring at me so tender I want to reach out and hold him.

"Whatever is between you and Will . . . it's . . . well, I can see it, okay? And Oliana can see it, too. Everyone on the island can see it, for the love of God."

And who comes up right behind Ku just now but *you damned well know who*? His face all pissier than thou, like he doesn't know exactly why I've been staying clear of him.

"Someone's been looking for you," I tell Will, trying my best to sound like my knees aren't about to give out right from under me.

"You don't say," he says, folding his arms. He's got a short-sleeved shirt on and the flames painted all over his skin look downright phosphorescent under the cloudy sky.

"You want to venture a guess as to who?"

"Not you, I imagine," he says.

"Neville," I say. "Dr. Cornelius Kandinsky Neville."

From the corner of my eye, I see Ku start to back away from us. I think I hear him say that he'll see me later, but I'm not sure, because in the next moment Will Tongahai goes and picks me up, throwing me over his shoulder like a sack of grain. My crutches fall to the ground and I try to catch my breath as he's practically knocked it all out of me. The damned crutches lay crisscrossed on the footpath like an X marks the spot and disappear from view altogether as Will marches right into the jungle brush that lines the back of all these thatched houses. The vines grab at me as he takes me further into the trees and the sweet, lush smell of island flowers envelopes us like expensive perfume. At the base of one of the smaller rock cliffs that leads up to the plateau, he finally puts me down.

"You think you're Tarzan or something?"

I barely get the words out before he kisses me, leaning

me against the rock face and letting out a groan. Or maybe that's me groaning. I don't know.

"Don't you ever push me away again," he says as we break.

"Push you away!" I say, pretty much gasping for breath. "You're the one who's got a girl. Who's had a girl all this time!"

Will closes his eyes and shakes his head. He takes me close, and I practically melt into him. Part of me wants to kick him and beat him and run away, but the other part of me . . . well, that's the one that's pathetic and simpering on the inside. The one that's in love with him. There, I said it. Thought it, anyway.

"She *was* my girl," Will whispers, putting emphasis on was. "We were so young. But she's not my girl now."

He kisses the top of my head and I breathe in the scent of his neck—all salt wind with traces of frangipani. Like he laid down in a field of flowers and took a long nap. I think it's the best smell in the world.

"Why not?"

Will takes my face in his hands.

"Why isn't she your girl anymore?" I ask him.

Will looks out into the little hash of jungle we're in. It's all dripping flora with the occasional furry fruit bat. Home to him. He caresses my head, like I'm dear and I watch him take a deep, long breath. The kind made of dreams and laments. I know it well.

"I was so sad leaving her at first," he says. "I've known Oliana all my life—from the times we used to play pirates together in the chasm, to when we got older and things changed. The Vakaafis are part of our *magafaoa* and every-one always told us we'd end up together. I never doubted it until I left the island."

It's hard for me to hear it, I won't lie. *Magafaoa*, the

extended family groups that make up the island culture here, are everything. They cook together and pray together, decide on inheritances and land ownership issues. They are the closest of the close, more than mere cousins, although not necessarily related by blood. I can almost hate Oliana for their memories, every first they gave to each other. I think Will must see my thoughts written all over my face.

"When I arrived at school on that first night," he tells me, "and I went to bed after the whirl of meeting everyone and unpacking my things; that's when I had the dream. The one I told you about. Of a pair of hands, a woman's." Will closes his eyes and licks his lips. "I woke up shaking and so thirsty. My heart felt like it had burst in my chest and I was sweating all over."

He steps away from me, gazing down the throat of a hot pink hibiscus that's grown up the side of the rock. It's like I'm losing him and I reach out to touch his arm, keep him with me. He takes my hand, making our fingers run together in a weave. It feels like our hands should always be this way. I bend down and kiss his knuckles. Each one.

"On other nights more dreams came; the most vivid pictures I could imagine," he says. "They tore at me, you see, like thorny weeds. I couldn't think of anything else. All of what you see inked on my body, Angelie. It's about a girl. One I'd never met before. But I saw her every night when I went to sleep."

Will turns back to me and untangles our hands. His fingers trail down my neck, pittering over my collarbone like the feet of a grasshopper.

"It's not that I didn't care about Oliana anymore after that. But I knew I wasn't in love with her—I wasn't meant to be somehow. I loved the girl in my stories. The ones I had painted on my body."

"I don't understand," I whisper.

"The night I met you. When the boat came in with the African and German scientists," Will says. "You're the girl. I was sure from the moment I saw you."

Will takes my hand and places it on his heart. It drums with a rhythm that feels less like a man's than the pulse of a whole universe.

"Will," I say. "What if I'm not that girl? What if you only think I am?"

Will shakes his head and holds my hand even closer. His heart is booming now, I feel it banging into the center of my palm.

"She had your eyes, Angelie. Like stained glass with the sun coming through." He bends down and kisses my brow. "And there was something else I knew when I fell into those eyes of hers."

"What?" I whisper.

"That whoever she was, she was dreaming of my eyes, too."

All at once, a strange electricity prickles the air. I feel as if I'll explode into a flight of birds, bits of me taking off in every direction. Even the hibiscus flower stands taller, straining and shuddering.

"Will," I say. His eyes, richer than the earth, more salient than the outrageous tapestry of his skin. They bring me inside him. Not just into his thoughts, which are plain, but into the very body of his soul. And yes, he's right. I have seen them. God help me—I remember now.

"You have to tell me," he says. "What have you been dreaming?"

Chapter 11

SAND HILLS of white and gold between small islands of soil and greenery, much the way Niue and her sister islands speckle the ocean. A complex of caves, like a city apartment building, with walls that glitter as if they've been sprayed with millions of diamond chips. Since I can remember, I've spent my nights among those caves and the people who inhabit them. Lying next to a young man.

I only know him by the way he touches me in the dark. His rough hands and soft feet. He calls me Sherin, saying my name like a prayer. The most familiar voice in all the world, in all of time. As intimate as the voice of God.

"It's you," I say, and Will kisses me as if answering.

My days were made of Sydney, and now they're made of Niue. But my nights have always been made of the other, with him.

Under the moon and stars, the only shared landscape of my days and nights, I have seen his eyes. As rich as chocolate, but with radiant streaks of amber, and deep winding rivers more red than roses or cherries or even ruby slippers. They've always been there, Will's eyes. Waiting for me. And I tell him so.

Will is glad to hear all of it. Because he wanted me to tell him, of course—that I feel the same way about him, I mean. But he's also relieved to hear he isn't mad as a hatter.

"*Ich denke, unsere beste Chance ist Vaikona.*"

A sentence as shrill as the clamor of broken pottery rips us away from our shared dreams. It's coming from beyond the dense web of forest, close to where we came in.

"Damned German bastards," I whisper, and Will gives me a look.

"They're with the Axis!" I tell him.

"Vogel and Neville?"

"Are you honestly surprised?"

Their steps rustle in closer, and they continue their menacing chit-chat in the enemy tongue.

"We should hide."

"Why?"

"Because they work for the Germans, that's why. And we can follow them and maybe find out what they're bloody up to."

Will is clearly unconvinced, and knits up his brows at me like what I'm saying is science fiction.

I look about for a good crag to hide behind, but Will picks me up, taking the lead and humoring me, at least. He knows this place, and brings us to an indent in the rock face, only a few steps away. He sets me down very gently, having me lean on him. If we stand flat against the limestone, they shouldn't be able to see us, provided they don't go looking.

Sure enough, Neville parts the wing-like fronds of a screw pine, and he and that Vogel bloke enter our little clearing. Vogel holds a map and a compass, and seems to be marking a route as he and Neville go on with that incomprehensible barking, pointing straight up the rope ladder that's been fixed to the rock. They start to climb, and in no time at all have reached the top, where they disappear from our view.

"What are you waiting for," I say, limping on over to the ladder. I try to step up onto the thing, but a shooting pain in my calf just about makes me double over.

"You can't climb that," he says. "At least not without help."

I punch at the limestone—not even very hard—but still have to flick little gravelly bits out of the shallow scrapes I've gone and given myself.

"Bloody damnation! They're getting away!"

Will takes my hand and blows on my silly injury. "It's alright," he says. "I know where they're going."

"How?"

Will tips his head.

"I may not speak much German, but they did say Vaikona at least three times, and that chasm happens to be located exactly in the direction they were pointing."

Vaikona, I mouth. Sounds like the name of a Norse queen.

"Is it far?" I look down at my leg, which is most certainly looking enflamed.

"Far enough that I won't let you walk it," Will says.

"What do you mean you won't let me? Don't you get it? They're in with Hitler and the bloody Nips! Ku and I saw them. That night we met at the plank, when we were walking home. They had a transmitter and were trying to contact a submarine, I know it!"

"How do you know? They could've been doing anything."

"But they weren't. I'm sure of it. You should've seen them—all guilty looking. Trying to get us to go away."

"Okay, but what would they want with a submarine here on Niue? We're pretty far away from the action. I mean, if this were Sydney, a submarine could at least do some real damage . . ."

Will stops and swallows. He takes my hand again, squeezing it. "I shouldn't have said that."

"It's fine," I tell him. "It was a long time ago."

He gives me a nod and bends down, taking a good right look at my leg. His fingers run gently over my stitches, which stick up like the bristly hairs along a hyena's spine. He curls his mouth up in a twist, flashing an expression that seems to confirm his worst expectations. Taking a good lungful, he goes upright again and offers me his back.

"You better hop on," he says.

"You expect to carry me on those feet? The ones all wrapped up in bandages?"

"I've got tough feet, you know. My dad says they came out of the womb as hardy as leather."

I look up the rock and cross my arms. Damn, I don't want those black hats to get away, but I don't want to hurt Will either. And carrying me on his back, walking on those feet will most definitely hurt.

"I know a short cut," Will says. "We might even get there before they do."

I put some weight on my leg, testing it out.

"Angelie, I'm going with or without you. Does that make your decision easier?"

This time I do gimp on over. I guess the least we can do for the war effort is spend a few uncomfortable hours in the chase of bad men. I climb on with some care and Will doesn't so much as wince.

"This seems to be the preferred method of carrying around injured young maidens on this island."

Will looks back at me, smiling. "Well, you're not a maiden anymore, are you?"

⊙

THE TRAIL UP TO VAIKONA chasm gets more and more jagged and absolutely snarled in growth with each labored step. Not that Will's laboring all that much, but I am, and feel a fool for panting so hard just from hanging on like a monkey.

Upon our approach, we find ourselves looking straight down into the chasm and I can't help but let out one of those horror movie gasps.

Positively medieval, it's huge and looks like a gothic castle in ruin. Not at all like it belongs on Niue, but in some creepy corner of Europe. I almost expect to find burnt corpses of heretics lining its outer walls as we wind our way to the back. There, the sides of the chasm ascend really high—maybe thirty five yards or more of murky gray, rugged rock—and the waves crash onto the spikey boulders at the base, making a deafening noise.

From here, Will's got to put me down, as I'll have to give it a go on my own, given the terrain. Inching along, we lower ourselves into a deep cave, aided by a thick fisherman's rope that's been hung from the top and makes navigating the giant rocks something less than a heroic feat. Will watches me close, afraid I'll slip or fall, and I can't say as I blame him. I want to show him I can do it, though, bum leg or no.

Once inside, it gets a bit easier and I'm able to make my way around without the beastly cohort of throbbing pain. I shamble over a stage of old, porous coral to its edge, where there are two crystal clear pools of water; ones filled with crayfish and black carp, or so Will tells me.

"Too right," I say.

Will drapes my arm across his shoulder, helping me favor my right leg, but the going is slower than I'd like. Vaikona is cavernous, and would take a mounted expedition to explore properly, but I assume Will has some good knowledge of the place. He takes us in deeper, into grottos that look like they could double for dungeons. I wonder if maybe those sinister blokes we're stalking aren't bringing Frankenstein to life somewhere on the premises. Just as a cherry on their wicked sundae.

"Shouldn't we be more careful," I say, bending over to give my leg a bit of a rub. "It's wide open in here and they could see us from a number of places."

"I could see you when you came in," Neville says, giving me such a fright I tip over and land onto my bum. He's standing on a short plateau that spreads out graciously from another cavern higher up. Like it's a balcony at a big theater or something.

"Dr. Neville," Will says all friendly. "There you are!"

Neville climbs down a crumbly path that made an accidental staircase when part of the chasm collapsed at some point. A thousand years ago for all I know. He's holding that statue of his and wears this happy smile that I find positively infuriating.

"I see you did find Will, after all," he says.

"Well, it's just thrillsville we all found each other, isn't it?"

Will puts out his hand and helps me up. Then he offers me his back again. Tempting as it is, I give him a firm *no*. Neville gives Will a look that says *good luck with that one*, and motions for us to follow him up from where he came. I grab the back of Will's shirt and pull him towards me.

"Just what do you think you're doing? I'm not going

anywhere with him," I whisper, though I'm quite sure Neville heard me.

"You're the one who wanted to come here," Will says.

"And you right know why!"

Neville clears his throat and the both of us stop and look at him.

"I fear we've come to some sort of misunderstanding."

"No bloody kidding!" I say, before Will can start trying all nicely to explain my behavior. Like I'm the one who's the problem! "Everyone else on the island may think you and that German bloke are just lovely and oh, so interesting, but I know what you're really up to."

Neville presses his lips together and loses all of his levity. At least he's finally done being a phony.

"Really?" he says. "Well, sometimes it takes an outsider to see what's plain, doesn't it?"

"Don't you patronize me."

"Patronize you? I'd never patronize you, Angelie."

Neville walks right up to me—close—and Will just lets him!

"Angelie," Neville says. "I want you to know that I take you deadly seriously."

The way he says *deadly* gives me a shiver.

"Angelie," Will says. "I think you should listen to what the man has to say."

Oh, God, I hope Will's not with them. He can't be, but he can't be this gullible either. Especially not after I told him about what Ku and I saw.

"Will, this bloke is a spy!"

Neville holds up his statue like it's an Oscar, which is the height of cosmic sarcasm.

"I'm an archaeologist," he says.

"That's what you seem to be, isn't it?" I say. "And maybe it's what you are, but you're something else, too, aren't you?"

Neville holds out the statue, bringing it close to my face. I inhale a sharp breath, holding it in, and a dew of sweat breaks out at my temples.

"I could say the same about you," he says, and touches the head of the statue to my neck.

A blinding current of God-knows-what blasts into my carotid artery and, given the quick jolt of pain and bizarre, rapturous feeling that accompanies it, I'm impressed I manage to remember the word carotid from my last year's biology lesson. Neville doesn't hold that thing there for more than a second or two, but in those moments, I swear I go elsewhere. I go well beyond the world that visits me in my dreams. It's the bright fuse of the heart of a great explosion, the Pyramid of Giza—from the inside, a dark and foggy night on a street in London—one with a carriage rumbling down it, not an automobile the way it would be today, and a storm coming over a black and craggy mountain in the desert. Out of breath, the whole cavern spinning around me, I see Will's face come closer. It's Will, but it's not Will. Darker skin and hair, a thinner face. The eyes. Oh, but the eyes are the same.

"*Ah'kwarah'a*," he says to me, and then it all goes black.

Chapter 12

"**M**Y GOD," I hear Neville say. "It's true."

I open my eyes to a dubious scenario. I'm standing high above them all on the nose of a bulbous, rocky growth jutting out from the cavern wall.

"How did I get here?"

"You climbed," Will says.

That seems not at all likely. I mean, yes, possible for someone without a deep gash in her leg—there are plenty enough divots to make for a good try—but not for me, and not today. Especially with no rope—I mean nothing—for help. I reach down to touch my wound and find it a bit sore, but I can put weight on it. I feel terribly self-conscious with everyone staring at me. Even Max Vogel has joined the party, standing behind Neville like he always seems to do. At his feet is that damned machine I saw on the night Ku and I caught them in their mischief. I notice it's not only a transmitter, but a recorder as well. I'd seen one of those on my dad's ship.

"Turn that thing off," I say.

Neville looks over his shoulder at Vogel and shrugs. The German bends down and flips the switch; the reels come to an unhurried stop.

I grab hold of the crags on the wall and slide down onto

my bum, intending to crab-crawl it, but Will tells me to stay right where I am. He's coming up.

"You mind telling me what this is all about?" I say. Will makes his way to me in no time and holds out his hand, helping me to my feet. Even he's looking at me awfully funny.

"I thought you had all the answers," Neville says, and Vogel seems to think that's just hilarious. Or as hilarious as a humorless Deutschenbloke like him can possibly find anything. He stands there smiling, a silent chuckle making his chest rattle. I shoot him the dirtiest look I know.

Will shows me to a bit of rock that's less of a vertical climb down. Sharp and irregular, yes, but at least it goes at a slope. That damned Neville comes up and holds his arms out to me.

"Go ahead, jump," he says, and I tell him that he must have lost his mind.

Will puts his arm around me and kisses my temple. "It's alright," he says. "He'll catch you."

I tippy-toe to the edge and take a good long gander at the African. He's strong, that's for sure. Tall and swarthy. And probably the only way I'm going to get down from here without breaking a leg—or breaking Will's.

"Geronimo," I say, and pitch myself into his out-stretched arms. With any luck, my weight will crush him to the ground. Give him some cuts and scrapes, though he deserves much worse. But no. He catches me with no problem at all and sets me down like I'm light as a doll. He even laughs about it.

Will makes way from our perch and stands next to me, putting his arm around me all protective again. But not like he's defending me from them. More like the way you treat someone fragile who's just had a bit of a shock. Then we all stand there looking at each other and I can't help feeling I've entered some sort of dark, secret society—with all of this being part of my initiation.

"What exactly is it you say is alright?" I tell Will. "That you're all cozied up with these two? Your Neville did something to me. I don't know what it is, but he did it that first night he came to the island, too. When he handed me that crook of a statue!"

Neville holds up the terrible little effigy, then passes it to Vogel. "It's just a figurine, Angelie. I can touch it. Max here can touch it. Only seems to have an effect on you."

"And me," Will says. "But it's not the same."

Will unwraps himself from me and walks over to Vogel, taking that thing from his hand. The moment he touches it, his face changes. His eyes fix like a blind man's and his movements stop, as if he's been frozen. Only his pulse and breath betray him.

I go to Will, standing close, so close he should feel the heat of my body. But it's as if he doesn't know I'm here.

"Get it away from him!" I say to Vogel. "For God's sake, take it away!"

Vogel wrenches the statue from Will's hand and he comes back to us, his shoulders relaxing, his eyes animating again. They dart around until they come upon me and he smiles.

"What did you see?" I ask him.

Will shakes his head.

"Nothing. It's not what I see, but what I know."

"What in the Devil's Triangle is that?"

He shrugs and looks over at Neville.

"My destiny."

I WALK AROUND their spy machine—recorder, transmitter, whatever it is—taking a good gander at the knobs and switches. All metal and wood, the thing looks like it belongs in the library of some shadowy millionaire.

"What the devil have you been recording in here?"

Neville and Vogel look to one another, and Vogel shakes his head, throwing a leery glance my way. Will steps forward and puts his hand on the thing, almost petting it.

"You, for one thing," he says.

"What do you mean me?"

Neville comes up and fidgets with the machine, running the reels backward. He gestures to one of the knobby coral stools.

"You may want to sit down," he says.

I look to Will, who nods. While part of me wants to tell Neville to go stuff it, just for the sake of telling him to go stuff it, there's another part that thinks it might be a really good idea for me to have a seat. For once, I follow "doctor's" orders. Will stands behind me and puts his hands on my shoulders, making me tremble a bit. It's a sweet and intimate gesture that makes me feel like I'm safe, as long as he's with me.

Vogel leans up against the rock wall, plucking a blue morning glory from a vine and twirling it in his fingers. Neville puts his finger on a flip switch. He takes a deep breath and smiles at me, compressing the lever. There's some static at first and the sound of voices in the background. Will's, Neville's. And another voice I don't recognize. Soft and earnest, formal in a way. I nearly fall off the rock when I realize it's mine.

"Nif," my voice says. And I wonder *what in the bloody hell is a nif.*

"*There is a wind in the desert that speaks of secrets. Yours and mine.*" There's an odd staccato to the way I'm speaking. It's not a way I've ever expressed myself before. I sound much older, like the young men who come back from the war. They leave with the ambition of performing courageous deeds, and come back with that ambition fulfilled. And all the terrible trophies that come with such a thing. Missing limbs, burns, ghosts. That's assuming they come back at all.

"*I think of our last hours together. Maybe it was only minutes. The storm coming to bury us in the desert. The way you held me, whispering stories into my ear. Of our child, of my home.*"

"Who am I talking to?"

Will takes my hand and looks into my eyes. There's a deep knowledge in his gaze, like there is in my voice on the recorder. "Me," he says. "You were touching my face. Then you kissed me."

There's a rumbling sound on the recording and it must be me climbing up the rocks.

"*It's strange how the fates have brought us here. When I look down upon this place, I see the Rah'a. The chasm wall rising up like the dunes, the stones that have been smoothed by the ocean tide roll like the sand of the desert floor. It's a map of my kingdom. If you stand where I am, it's as if you're at the top of the dunes, and can look east to that twist of coral rock, as if you're looking to where the Palace City would be—right beneath a large plateau of limestone.*"

I look at Neville and his eyes are alight. I can hear his breath, as excited as if he's watching a naked girl dance.

"Are you saying that right here, where we're standing . . .

that this is a map of the Kingdom of Rah'a?" Neville inquires of my voice.

"What's the Kingdom of Rah'a?" I ask, but Will shushes me.

"*You look so much like your father,*" my voice says. "*A great man he was. The best friend I could ask for.*"

"You weren't talking to me anymore right then," Will whispers. "You were addressing Neville."

I look back at the African bloke and he meets my eyes, smiling at me in that kindly uncle way again. Biting down on my lip, I turn back to the recorder like it's a person or something.

"*It all awaits us beneath the desert floor,*" my voice says. I can hear Neville ask "What is it?" on the recording.

"*I don't know,*" my voice says. "*I don't even think Nif knows, although I suspect there's plenty he hasn't told me over the centuries. I can hardly fault him for that, as I've kept my own secrets.*"

There's a long pause on the recording. I can hear a bird cawing in the background and the collective breath of Will, Neville and Vogel.

"*Everything you need to find the Rah'a is here. This is your map room. Nif and I are your guides. In this life and the next. However long it takes.*"

Chapter 13

"**DID HE HYPNOTIZE ME** or something?" I demand of Will. He opens his mouth as if to answer, but doesn't.

I limp on over to Neville and point my finger right into his chest. "You black-hearted fiend, did you hypnotize me?"

Neville tries to take my hand, but I push him, and the big bloke hardly moves. All along he's got that look of *oh, you poor thing* on his face. Like I'm his long-lost daughter.

"I know what a shock this must be," Neville tells me. "I've been hearing of this all my life, yet it's a shock to me. And I'm not even a . . ."

"A what?"

Neville reaches out to touch my face, his fingers firm and soft like swan feathers against my cheek. His breath hitches, and he holds his eyes very wide.

"A Nin'ti," he whispers.

"A Nin'ti!" I step back and put my palms to my temples—a lame effort to get a hold of myself. "Have you gone mad? Have you all up and lost your bloody minds!"

"Those vivid dreams you've talked about," Neville says. "Are they not filled with what's on that recording?"

I swallow hard and glance at that filthy Nazi, Max Vogel. He's gaping at me with a dog-eyed wonder that makes me want to smack his face.

"What would you know about my dreams? Either of you!"

"Exactly," Neville says. "I only met you a couple of weeks ago. Maybe Max and I could figure out how to trick you here on Niue. With drugs or hypnosis. But are we accountable for what you've been dreaming all your life?"

"I don't know what you're accountable for, but I do know damned well it's no good. I'm a Nin'ti you say? Well you're both Nazis!"

"*Sherin,*" I hear from behind me.

Good God. His voice moves through me like high voltage. It's Will, yes, but at the same time it's not. So serious—full of devotion. Damned frightening. And so damned loving it makes me want to cry.

"Will?" I ask.

Against all my better judgement I turn around. Will stands there, the statue in his hand. His shoulders are back and his neck extended, longer it seems—or maybe it just looks that way from how he's holding himself. Like he's more slender, but still powerful. As if he's used to being obeyed. The strange thing is his eyes. Exactly like when he last touched the statue. It's as if he's standing in pitch darkness and can't see me. I walk up to him, waving my hand in front of his face, but he doesn't register it at all.

"Who are you?" I ask him.

"*I'm the one who loves you, and has sworn to protect you in every life we live.*"

He's so still. I lean in to him and take in the scent of his skin right at his neck, where I love it most. But he doesn't smell like Will at all. There's a dustiness to him, the vague smell of burnt nuts. A musk that would never form on a man in a lush place like Niue.

"Why?"

Will's lip curls up a bit, a look I've seen on his face and one he shares with this . . . whatever, whoever.

"Because it is our destiny. What I swore to you on the day we wed and what I have promised to the one who made us."

"Who is that?" I whisper.

Feels rather sacrilegious to ask, right? I mean who else would make us other than God? But then in the midst of this complete and utter lunacy, I wouldn't be surprised if he said Bette Davis.

"Sherin," he says. There's some urgency in his voice.

"There is a man named Harry Ainsley. He has a message for you."

The statue falls from Will's hand, dropping onto the rock floor with a hollow clunk. Will takes a whopping breath and swallows, his eyes focused again. Himself again.

I throw my arms around him, holding him tight. So glad to have him back with me, and yet already missing the other. I kiss his shoulder. Everything feels wet as we stand there in an embrace of sweat and tears. I run my hands up his back just to feel something familiar—something I knew before all of this hocus pocus started. Through his shirt, I come upon the stitched up cuts from when he carried me over the hot-orange coral.

"Will," I say.

I break away from him, backing up to one of the knobby stools where I sit down again. Folding my hands, I bow my head and say a quick but fervent prayer. Like I did so many times right after Dad and Jay were killed, just to get through the day. When I open my eyes again, Will is standing before me. Neville and Vogel are behind him, curious and a tad awestruck at the drama unfolding.

"Will," I say again. "I need you to take off your shirt."

(())

HE UNBUTTONS from the collar down in a determined flow of motion, then slips the shirt off his shoulders and lets it fall to the ground. Neville's all watchful, staring at Will's back in fascination. His mouth drops open and he starts to shake his head.

"You've seen his back before," I say. "You're the one who stitched him up."

Neville swallows and licks his lips. He walks up close to Will and dabs his fingers over the scars like he's not quite sure what's going to jump out of them.

"Are they not healing properly?" Will asks.

"They're healing perfectly," Neville tells him, his voice fraught with that sense of confusion and marvel that's been the rule of the day. Only doubly so.

"But they've changed."

"What do you mean?" I ask him.

"Will had several cuts, some very deep, and others, more superficial, that crisscrossed over one another," he whispers.

I remember his back at Oliana's, practically varnished in blood. He had to have a dozen cuts at the very least.

Neville takes his eyes away from Will's back and meets mine. "Now there are two. One like a lightning bolt, and the other curled like a snail shell. It's as if the lacerations moved and joined one another."

"Surely, that's not possible," Will says, sounding more like me by the moment. He turns around, giving me the gander that I asked for, and moves his braid into a coil round his neck. He squints over his shoulder at me, his face above the girl with my eyes.

Will's back is fully glorious again, a heroic poem from the blue blood moon at the nape of his neck all the way to the desert night it shines down upon. Flanking his spine are the two arrows, just like before. Only now, next to those, are the new shape-shifting scars that just about knocked Neville to the ground. The bolt of lightning on one side, as crisp as if it came out of a thundercloud. And the spiral on the other, so precise as to appear as if it was made using a math compass.

"No bloody way," I say.

"Lightning imagery is found in almost every human mythology," Neville murmurs. "It's most often a weapon of justice. Instant retributive destruction."

"And the curly-cue?" I ask him.

"They're some of the oldest shapes in the ancient world, dating back as far as the Neolithic period. And they are the most potent symbols of creation known to man."

"Neolithic," I say. "Cave people, you mean? Is that how old you think we are?"

Neville shakes his head. "Not quite. The Rah'a, assuming now that it did indeed exist, was a very advanced civilization that would have been wiped out before the rise of the Sumerians."

"Wiped out? How?"

Neville takes a deep breath and puts his fists on his hips. "I don't know, and I won't know until we uncover its remains. Max here thinks it was buried by a sandstorm."

"That must've been one helluva storm," Will says.

"Ja," Vogel grunts. "If the geological samples I've found in the Sahara are any indication, it would have lasted for years."

It's all a lot to take in, and I'm not quite sure I believe it. There has to be some rational explanation for all of this.

We're in the twentieth century, for the love of God, and I would hope we've moved beyond the age of mythology.

"So, you two," I say to Neville and Vogel. "How long have you been chasing after this 'Rah'a'?"

Neville throws his head back in a bold laugh, deep as a bass solo.

"Me?" He says. "Angelie, the Nevilles have been hunting the Rah'a for decades. As for Max . . ." Neville slaps the German's gut. "Max joined me, when? Near on seventeen years, isn't it? We were only about your age, girl."

Max Vogel nods.

"And how long have you known about this?" I ask Will.

He turns to me fully and comes over, taking my hands. "When did I believe it? Only today, actually. But Dr. Neville, he . . ."

"When I cleaned up young Will's back after your shark incident—that's when I was sure," Neville cuts in. "You see, the picture inked onto his back, it was the first time I'd seen it on him, but not the first time I'd seen it."

"What do you mean?"

"I mean I know this place." Neville steps toward Will and points to the hills of night-blue sand that meander across the small of his back. "We've stood right here, haven't we Max? And I can tell you in language I think you'll appreciate, Angelie. It's a damned hellish bugger of a place to get to."

I place my hand on Will's back and he startles. My finger rides along the lines of a soaring dune inked into his side.

"Who is Harry Ainsley?" I ask.

Will blinks in confusion.

"You said Harry Ainsley has a message for me. When you were holding that statue. Seeing your destiny, I imagine."

Will takes a breath and shakes his head. He crosses his

arms and walks behind Neville and Vogel, doing a lap of the "map room," as my voice called it.

"Harry Ainsley was my friend. Is my friend, I should say."

The statue is tucked back into Neville's holster and Will eyes it. "I knew Harry at school, and he conspired with me to join the war. See, he was just about to turn eighteen and his father is an Admiral in the Royal Navy. Figured slipping in with him was a shoe-in, but, uh, he was able to join and I wasn't."

"It was your roommate who ratted you out," I say. "That's what I heard, at least."

Will looks up at me.

"Yes," he says, shutting tight those eyes of his. "Only Harry was my roommate."

"Your Harry? Why would he do that?"

Will glances down at his hands as if they might provide an answer.

"To this day I don't know."

Will's eyes follow the flames up his arm and caress the woman on the other. He grazes his hands along the upside down sunrise on his chest. "Harry tried to talk me out of going to the inkmaster at first. Thought I was full-on mad. But after I'd been a couple of times, he started coming with me. We talked endlessly about the dreams I was having."

Will goes and picks up his shirt.

"Thought he was the best friend a guy could have."

Neville comes up and puts his hand on Will's shoulder. His eyes glitter in that wet way of his. Dark as a deep lake nestled in a crater.

"Will," he whispers. "I think Max and I may be able to provide some answers for you."

"About Harry Ainsley?" I say.

Neville nods.

"Has Will talked about him before? I mean when he held that statue of yours?"

Neville reaches up and strokes the wings of the little figure. He shakes his head.

"A young man named Harry Ainsley, an officer in the British Navy as it were, is the man with whom we've been in contact," he tells us.

Will digs his fingers into his hair, his eyes wide as gooseberries. "Harry! The Harry I know?"

Neville shrugs and licks his lips. "I can't say for sure, obviously. Only way to know would be to ask him. But it seems serendipity has taken us all in her passionate embrace of late. My money says that our Harry Ainsley is your Harry Ainsley. But then I am a man born of a superstitious people. And I'm a betting man, too."

Max Vogel puts his hand on their machine.

"It was Harry Ainsley we were transmitting messages to on the night you and Ku stumbled into us. He's stationed on a British submarine patrolling these waters."

"And what do you want with him?" I ask.

Neville purses his lips and looks me and Will over.

"Oh, come on," I say. "I think we're past the point of keeping secrets, don't you? And who the devil do you think we'd tell?"

Neville peers over at Max and they fix their eyes on each other in that wordless way they have of communicating. Mum and Aunt Kitty can do that, but then they're twins.

"It's a bit of triangulation, is all," Neville tells us. "Our small part for the war effort, Max and mine. See, Angelie, we really are scientists. But we're also men and patriots. Max here, is an American. And so am I. Not by birth, but by choice."

"American," I say. "Then what are you doing here?"

Neville takes the statue out of his holster again, and I flinch. He smiles, placing it on the machine, where it stands, deviant, as if flouting all conventions of time and space.

"This is what we're doing here, just as I told you. By way of University of Chicago, where Max and I are fellows. And Harry Ainsley is what we're doing while we're here by way of the Allied Alliance."

"Allies," I say. Now there's a kick in the head.

Neville comes over and sits down on one of the coral lumps next to me. Looks like he means to take my hand, but he doesn't. I glance up at Will and he shrugs his shoulders.

"Go on," I say.

Neville's nostrils twitch as he collects his thoughts. Finally, he meets my eyes, his gaze so keen I can almost feel it touch me.

"For some years now, the British Navy has been hunting a Japanese submarine known only as *Akuma*," he tells me. "She sweeps in stealth-like and torpedoes Allied destroyers. Then just disappears."

"The British think it's possible *Akuma* was part of the attack on Sydney Harbor," Vogel elaborates.

My legs break into a queer, prickly tingle and I have to stand up. I want to move, pace about, but I feel stuck to the ground like a barnacle. In a flash, my skin grows all cold and I swear every drop of blood drains from my face, making me feel queasy. I sit down again, nearly missing my perch this time, but Will reaches out and steadies me.

"Those were Ko-hyoteki-class midget submarines," I say. "Just two man subs. I read all about them."

"Yes," Neville tells me. "But they came from somewhere

and it's unlikely they could have done all that damage on their own. Their mother ship must have swept in and given them a hand."

My throat closes up on me and Will grips my hand, squeezing it tight. I feel like I'm there again, back in Sydney on the day it all started. The teachers whispering to one another, some of them bursting into tears. Then Sister Josephine coming in and telling us to all go home. Saying everything's going to be all right. God's got a plan. But I didn't go home. I went to the harbor, hitching a ride from a woman with a white stripe in her hair. It's all I remember about her. She was going for the same reason I was, I think, though we didn't say a word the whole way there. All the time I knew, I just knew, I would never see my dad again. That my life would never be the same.

"What's the story with all of those scars on Max's back?" I whisper. I see Max Vogel stiffen out of the corner of my eye.

Neville stands up and turns to his friend, putting his hands on his hips like he does. There's a look on the African's face I've only ever seen before on one person in the world. It was Mum after Dad went down, and then Jay. It's a look of such profound sadness and regret that it damn near breaks my heart. I guess I wasn't sure he was telling the truth about all of this until just right now when I asked about Max's scars. My eyes flit up at Will and he's watching Neville, too. Then he goes and does what I haven't the courage to do—he meets eyes with Max Vogel, and asks him to tell us.

Max Vogel doesn't move. He doesn't even take a deep breath like I would do before answering such a question.

"We were in North Africa when the Western Desert Campaign began," Max says. "And I had the misfortune of running into my brother. Hadn't seen him in years, but I knew what he'd become. Can't say I was surprised."

Neville rubs his palm over his five o'clock shadow, making a scritchety-scratch sound that almost mimics the susurrating murmurs of the ocean outside.

"Spent three days with my brother," Max says. "Until Kandi found me. Killed my brother and took me away. Tended my wounds when I told him to leave me to die. The Nazis would be hunting us after that, you see, and they did. But Kandi slipped us onto a boat to Turkey."

"Your brother was a Nazi officer," I say. "Who'd come with Rommel to North Africa?"

Max Vogel nods.

"He called me a traitor and, from his perspective, I am. Told me I deserved to die slowly. But that's not why he did to me what he did, Miss Angelie. He did it because he enjoyed it. Some people are like that."

A hard and heavy silence falls on the map room. I want to tell Max I'm sorry, that I was so wrong, but I don't really think he'd appreciate such a sentiment right now. Max Vogel, I think, just wishes to flush away all the suspicion and conclusions that have been drawn by his very existence. His German-ness. And to forget everything that ever happened between him and his brother, too, I imagine.

"When is it you're supposed to contact this Harry Ainsley again?" I say, and everyone seems right relieved at the change of subject.

Neville saunters over to the twisted rock my recorded voice claims is a representation of some ancient palace city.

"We next talk to Harry on the night of Will's hair cutting ceremony, 2:00 am sharp. And I think you both best be there."

A week from Saturday. So close it feels like it could be

tomorrow. Or in a thousand years. Time has lost all meaning to me.

"We'll be there," Will says.

"Too right," I tell them.

Chapter 14

THE DEEP WATER is as clear as a pane of glass. Will slices through it like an eel, then floats above the colorful brains of coral, looking as brilliant as any exotic sea animal. Reflected light flickers over the stories on his body. Diving deeper, he plucks a perfect spotted shell from the sea floor and swims to me. We break the surface of the water and I push my goggles up onto my forehead. Will, who doesn't need any, blinks the salt water out of his eyes, then leans in to kiss me.

Our mesh sack of shells clinks as we wade up to Hio beach, one of the only sandy beaches on Niue. White and soft as silt, the sand molds to our backs as we lie down and gaze up at a perfect sky that mimics the aqua blue of the ocean. I wonder how many times Will and I have seen such a vista together, in how many lives, and if we were as happy as we are right in this moment.

Will rolls onto his side and bends over me with that smile on his face. He kisses my neck.

"Again?" I say.

"You don't want to?"

"No, I do."

I brush the sand off his shoulder and press my lips to his skin. So soft, and brown as a glass of sherry.

"I'm thinking," I say. "God maybe doesn't mind that we

do this so often. Or at all. You did tell me—when you had that statue in your hand—that you promised to protect me from the day we were wed. God only knows how long ago that was. We could be celebrating our six-thousandth wedding anniversary, after all. I think when you look at it that way, we did wait until we were married, whether we knew it or not."

"Is that your Catholic rationale?"

"That's my story and I'm sticking to it." I slap his bum and he slaps me right back. "Though I doubt it's one Mum and Aunt Kitty would buy. If they knew what we were up to, they'd have me on the next boat back to Sydney."

Will gets all serious all of a sudden. "Well, we can't have that."

I reach up, touching the crossed swords with the gilded handles that lay just under his collarbone.

"They're Spanish," he says. "I dreamt in Spanish for a while back at school. Harry found a drawing of one of these actually. In an old, hand-written history book." He places his hand on mine, riding with it along the lines of his tattoo. "This particular style belonged to a family of Conquistadors."

"More Catholics," I say, stroking the handles. They're shaped like crucifixes and each is engraved with a family crest at the center.

"I think they were ours, these swords," Will tells me. "One from my family and the other from yours."

I look closely and do see that each crest is different. One has a lion and a castle and the other a bird of some sort. A rather fierce bird. That one has a sun, too.

"Do you think we've been married in every life?"

Will takes my hand from his swords and puts it down

right over where my heart beats, holding it there. "Don't know. Does it matter to you?"

I take a deep breath and look up at the sky. A tiny puff of a cloud has appeared and makes its way across the belly of the sun. "Yes," I tell him.

"Matters to me, too," Will whispers.

He rolls onto me, but doesn't go to kiss me right away this time. Just looks at me, and I at him. I want to do this all day, gaze at him, chart his every feature, memorize the startling hues that whirl in his eyes.

He hooks his finger under the strap of my bathing suit and begins to tug it down. "This time," he says. "I want to call you Sherin."

"Please," I say.

Every time he says that name, my name, I feel the call of a thousand angels.

"Sherin." He breathes the name onto my skin, kissing down towards my hip, pulling my bathing suit with him. "Sherin."

⟨⟩

WILL WALKS ME HOME, kissing me behind the wild shrubbery that grows like tangled hair just behind our house. Our house. It's the first time I've really felt it's my home and not just some place I'm staying in, was practically dragged to. Sydney, which I hated leaving with every fiber of my being, feels as far away as a distant planet right now. I don't think I care if I ever lay eyes on it again.

"I'll see you tonight," Will says. We hold each other, not at all wanting to be apart. Not even for a few hours. With a sweet reluctance, we break away, leaving only our two fingers hooked together. He leads me into our yard.

"Wear your purple dress," he whispers, before letting go his finger and starting back for his place, all long strides with a light wind in his hair.

"I dare you not to turn around!" I say, and he does right then, laughing. I blow him a kiss and he runs to me, giving it back wet and wonderful. "Run along now," I tell him, and this time he does go, pulling a long blade from a tuft of elephant grass and whipping it about as he walks.

Inside, our house is cool and aired out. The blinds are rolled half-way down, and blocks of shadow are pressed all over our furniture like an industrial skyline. There's a faint smell of roasted fish in the air, coming from our neighbors *umu* pit, and another smell, too.

"Your mum let me in," Oliana says from behind me. "Said I could wait for you. She went to Rose's house to make chutney with the women."

I turn around to face her rather carefully, so that she can't tell she scared me to death.

"Hello," I say.

Oliana is standing in the corner, wearing a prim cotton dress the color of a ripe green olive. Her long wavy hair looks blue-black in the afternoon light and she holds the bottle of Evening in Paris I gave her. For a moment I think she's going to chuck it at me, but she doesn't. She only puts it down on our brekkie table, then steps back as if it might blow up at any time.

"Oliana," I say. "I wanted you to have it."

"I know."

She walks over to the window and lifts up the shade a bit more, looking out onto the patch of short grass where Will and I said our goodbyes. She must have been watching

from here and I feel bloody awful about it. When I imagine
Will with Oliana it just about makes me want to shatter
every piece of glass I can lay my hands on, and roll in the
broken bits.

"You're coming to Will's ceremony, I hear."

A roar starts in my ears. The kind that rears up whenever
I hear my mum crying alone. I guess I'm hating myself
even though I know Oliana's broken heart isn't my fault.

"I'm sorry," I say, and she turns her head back toward
me.

"You know, the *hifi ulus*—hair cutting ceremonies—are
usually for close family and friends, which I guess is just
about everyone on this side of the island. Everyone but
you."

I swallow and look down at Oliana's sandals. A fine pair
that looks like they came from Bon Marché. Rose Tongahai
probably got them for her.

"I could have asked the Tongahias not to invite you," she
says, plucking Rose's name straight from my mind. "And
they wouldn't have. Out of respect for me and my parents."

I nod, not very inclined to speak just now.

"I didn't figure it would do me much good, though,"
she says.

"No, I suppose not," I manage.

Oliana looks me up and down, comparing the two of us,
I'm sure. Wondering what I have that Will wants and why
he doesn't want her anymore. I wish I could tell her it has
nothing to do with her at all. She thinks she's known Will
a long time, forever as far as she's concerned. She's watched
him grow tall and has waited all her life for tonight. The
night Will gets his hair cut and becomes a man in the eyes
of everyone on Niue. Her man. All these years have been
hers, but many more have been mine.

"I didn't know about you and Will," I tell her. "Not at first. I expected you and I would become friends."

Oliana walks back over to our brekkie table and picks up Evening in Paris. She opens the top and sniffs it, then dabs a little bit on her neck and wrists, before putting it back.

"What are you? Where did you come from?"

Her questions make the roar in my ears grow that much louder.

"Oliana, I didn't even want to come to Niue."

"No, but now that you have, you'll never leave will you?"

I bite down and shake my head.

Oliana turns her back to me and walks into the tiny ante-room where I sleep. She sits down on my cot and runs her hands along my covers—the ones we brought with us from Sydney. Then she lays down, fitting into the berth just as I do. We're very similar in form, I notice. Both with slight bones and breasts just a bit too generous for our frames. Well-defined faces. And we're practical women, the two of us, but only at a glance. We hold our emotions inside until we just can't anymore. After that, anything goes.

"I don't know what brought you here," Oliana whispers. "But you're not what I thought you were."

"Few of us are what people think we are," I tell her. "Sometimes we don't even know ourselves."

She props herself up onto her elbows and cranes her neck. A tiny moth flutters about in a stream of light just above her head like a little fairy. She looks up and waves it away.

"They like you, the Tongahais. They like you fine. But they love me."

"Of course they do," I say. "And Will, he loves you. He always will."

Oliana stands up from the cot and comes over to me, standing close and eye to eye. For a moment, I'm a little frightened of her, but then she softens. Her shoulders fall with her expression, leaving a young woman of dashed hopes before me.

"Green used to be my favorite color," she says.

She takes one more look out the window, to the spot where she saw Will and me kissing, and steps away. I take my first breath in what feels like a long time.

Watching her move towards the front door, wounded and cat-like, I can't help but remember the widows who came to the funerals of the men who died at the hands of the Jap subs. There was a whole group of them who went from funeral to funeral, saying little, bathing themselves in a shared sorrow. They came to Dad's funeral, and again to Jay's. Mum told me how she just wished they would go away. I didn't, though. I knew why they had come. Same reason Oliana came here today.

Oliana opens the door, letting in the dense afternoon air, heavy with a coming rain shower. One that's fast and hard, then opens up into a glorious evening. The kind that has everyone up late, singing and telling stories. Reveling in all that is good.

"I hate you," she says, before slipping out into those first tentative drops.

Chapter 15

MUM, AUNT KITTY AND I step up onto Will's porch and I'm glad they've come with me to the Tongahai home this time. I know how much Will wants me here, but after Oliana's visit, I'm not sure his parents feel as rosy.

The yard is empty, as the hair cutting ceremony will take place in the house, but the bonfire is set to be lit, there's a pig on a spit, and fish and fruit bats roasting in the *imu* pits. Rose's Kadupul flower, the one I helped nurse from a bit of root rot, sits in the windowsill. Seems rather expectant by the looks of her and I'm sure she'll bloom any night now. I hope that's a good sign.

Mum knocks and I can hear a lot of talk inside. Footsteps, sure and ladylike click behind the door until Rose Tongahai answers, her pleasant, English smile offered to the three of us like a gift.

"So good to have you back. The mango jam is a smash!" Rose says to my mother. They'd been canning here together for most of the day.

Aunt Kitty reaches out and Rose kisses her cheek, telling her she's starting to get a good bit of color, which I don't see at all. Then she turns to me.

"Angelie, dear," she says. "Lovely as a fresh plum, and just as sweet."

She puts out her hand and I take it, letting her lead me into the foyer, which is filled with fresh flowers of just about every variety I've seen on the island.

"Do go and get some refreshments," she tells us, opening the French doors to her living room. It's utterly packed with guests in there and so busy no one even looks to see who's arrived.

"Will shall make his appearance any time now," Rose says. "He's still getting ready."

I've never actually been inside Will's house until now. There's a casual elegance to the way it's been decorated—at once lively in the way of island homes, but a bit serious too. There are a few antiques that must have come from Rose's family, and it's an odd mix and match that somehow manages to work.

"How nice," Mum says, admiring a sideboard that's got to be a good hundred years old. Not that I know a thing about old furniture. It's all polished and perfect with delicate legs and the prettiest swirls in the wood. A spread of English tea sandwiches covers just about every inch of its top.

Mum and Aunt Kitty get swallowed up into the crowd right away, like they've lived here all their lives, while I stand about feeling like I've come to the wrong house. Mr. and Mrs. Vakaafi are nowhere in sight, which is a relief. No Oliana either. I can't even spot Ku, who's always at the center of any gathering, telling his stories and eating with a gusto that spreads like measles.

"Angelie!"

For the first time since my arrival on Niue, I'm happy to see Kandi Neville. Max Vogel is not in tow and I wonder if he isn't out getting things ready for our late night adventures regarding one Harry Ainsley, who may or may not be Will's roommate from school and the bearer of otherworldly messages for me.

"Ah, what a vision," he says. "Has anyone ever told you that lilac is your best color?"

"My mother, for one," I say, and he tips his head back in a hearty laugh.

"Kandi!" Nukai Tongahai calls out to him. "How about another rum punch?"

Mr. Tongahai sees me and nods. Polite, but not much more than that. He points to the punch bowl, and I nod back, happy to accept.

"Can I ask you something?" I say to Dr. Neville.

"Angelie, if you asked me for my first born, I might be tempted to give him to you."

I roll my eyes. "Charmer," I say.

Dr. Neville bows, then picks up my hand, kissing my knuckle ever so gently.

"Your name is right curious. All English and Russian, when you don't look to be either."

He lets go of my hand and stands up tall, tipping his head and puckering those full lips of his.

"Are you up for a story," he asks me.

I tell him I sure am. The longer the better. Anything to pass this awkward time until Will turns up. I don't tell him that part, though.

"My name is quite the family matter," he begins by saying.

He offers his elbow and takes me to a high-backed sofa as green as the ferns that drip from just about everywhere outside. We sit down and a young lad, one of a hundred little brothers running around, hands us the rum punches Mr. Tongahai promised. Neville takes a nice, long sip.

"You see, my grandfather was a very accomplished

British drinker. A true lout, and a charmer I might add, who traveled from country to country in search of his next glass of gin. And his next warm bed. One he found with my grandmother before setting off for the horn of Africa, never to return."

"I'm sorry," I say.

"I'm not." Neville crosses his legs at his ankles and looks deep into his punch. "A name, after all, is everything."

"Really?" I say. I've never thought so. The name, Angelie, has always been a bit of a stranger to me. Even my mum told me how she and my dad had fought about what to name me until the very minute I was born. They only settled on Angelie because our parish priest, a right rascal named Father Angel, had suggested it.

"You see, cad that he was, he did stick around long enough to give us his name. A good English name goes a long way in Africa. But it was my father who altered our destiny."

"How so?"

Neville leans his forearms onto his thighs, as he tends to do when thinking soberly, I've noticed. "He left Senegal for Egypt where he began our family quest for the ancient."

He squints one of his eyes at me like a jeweler would do when assessing the quality of a gem.

"I should preface this by saying that my grandmother also had quite a hand in our fate," he continues. "She blessed our family with names as well. Pixi—that's what we called her—she had the heart of an adventuress, and ran away to Paris when she was only fourteen. There, she studied under Rodin, though not formally. She met my grandfather, the lout, upon her return to Senegal when she was barely twenty. And when she gave birth to my father, she named him Cornelius Pissarro Neville."

He lifts up his rum punch in salute. "All the men in my family are Cornelius Neville. And all of us are given an artist's name in the middle."

"Pissarro, you say? Not Rodin?"

Neville smiles big and wide, like he's recalling a past romance.

"Pixi adored Rodin. In fact, he gave her a small sculpture that he created in her likeness. I keep it in a vault at my bank in Chicago."

Neville stretches and rubs his eyes with great satisfaction before settling down again. He takes a tea sandwich from a serving plate going around.

"Another sculpture?" I say. "You seem to collect those in your family. Must be worth a fortune, that one."

"Indeed. But luck is worth more."

He reaches under his arm to where his holster usually is. Where the ancient statue, my statue as I've come to think of it, often sits in place of a pistol. It's not there now and I feel a little sad for its absence, even if I have no inclination to touch it again.

"You still haven't told me why your grandmother named her son Pissarro then."

"Ah, well, that's simple. She obtained a dog from Pissarro and that little creature was her beloved companion until he was run over by a carriage only days before my father was born."

I sit back for a moment, laying my head against the wood-framed rest on the high back of the sofa. The room is loud and musty and full of island smells. My head is full of Nevilles.

"And your father," I say. "I take it he was a fan of Kandinsky's? Or did he buy a dog from him as well?"

"My father met Wassily Kandinsky in Moscow the year

I was born. Kandinsky believed all forms of art were able, quite equally, to reach a level of spirituality that even religion had trouble accessing. My father believed archeology was one part art and another part science. It was his religion. The two of them wrote letters to one another for years, and when my father died, I took up his correspondence."

"You write to Wassily Kandinsky?"

"Once a month without fail. And next time, I shall write to him about you."

I shake my head.

"Dr. Neville," I tell him. "You are a right, interesting man. I'll give you that."

Rose starts to hum an island song; one I don't really know. I expect it regards the hair cutting ceremony, as I recognize the Niuean word for it—*hifi ulu*. From behind me, Mr. Tongahai taps my shoulder and asks me to follow him. I look back at Dr. Neville and he flutters his hand, urging me to go along.

There's a big, copper urn in the corner, filled with a giant fern that seems to stand there and sway with its arms out like a priestess. It's a prime spot, and Mr. Tongahai deposits me next to it.

The humming grows louder as more people join in. It's a sweet and festive sound, but not unserious. There's a purpose to the beat that seems to speak of more than mere pleasure.

Mr. Tongahai begins to clap and I look over to the French doors, where Will has appeared. I nearly burst out laughing when I see him, and put my palm right square over my mouth to shut me up.

There he stands, his long hair beribboned and somehow managing to look utterly handsome and ridiculous all at once. He shoots me a look, but it's not cross. Will knows quite well what he looks like to an outsider like me.

Behind him are the Vakaafis, including Oliana and Ku. Oliana stares straight ahead, but Ku gives up a smile for me. They're all in their Sunday best, looking as casually English and islander as Rose Tongahai's house. What with flowers in the women's hair and their button-up dresses. The men in high-waisted pants and matching shirts tucked in, but also those sandals everyone here wears; the ones made of braided palm leaves and cork.

Rose and Mr. Tongahai take up on each side of Will and walk him to the sofa, which Dr. Neville has vacated. He's come to the other side of the fern and stands watching this ritual as anyone of his interests would—like he's observing a forgotten tribe in some Godforsaken jungle somewhere. His eyes are wide and wet and his lips are parted. He looks on with an undisguised sense of wonder as Will sits right in the middle of the green sofa and the women and girls gather around him.

"The women take care of a boy's hair until his *hifi ulu*," Ku whispers. He's come up next to me, too, and I'm glad for his company.

"Of course with Will, that's been a no go. He hasn't let a woman touch his hair since well before he left for England. Except for Oliana, of course."

That just about stabs me through the eye.

"Of course," I say.

Sure enough, Oliana takes up the scissors and lifts up one of Will's ribbon-wrapped locks. She takes a first snip right above where the ribbon is tied up top and holds it high for everyone to see. There's a big cheer and Will meets my eyes, so I swallow hard and give him the best and biggest smile I'm able. This is his day and I'm not about to behave like a jealous harpy.

One by one, each of the women and girls take a turn

cutting off a beribboned lock of Will's hair—something they get to keep for themselves as a memento of the occasion, and symbol of their role in making a man of Will.

I bite down on my lip as each tress of his hair is taken down. I've grown to love his strange, long hair. That it makes him look like he's from another world. But part of me is excited for the change, too. That the long hair is the old Will and the Will with his short, manly hair will be just for me.

As the girls gather around him, waiting their turn for the scissors, it becomes harder and harder for me to see what's going on. I hear plenty of *ooos* and *aahs,* lots of giggles, that's for sure. Even Rose gives up a hoot here and there. It's only Oliana who stands watching without so much as a smile. She clutches the ribbon-wrapped lock of Will's hair like a talisman, and I can swear that she's praying. Oliana never once looks my way.

Finally, the flurry around Will subsides and the girls stand there looking at him. I rise up on my tip-toes to see, but it's impossible to get even a glimpse of the new Will. That is, until he rises up from the couch.

I actually forget to breathe.

While his hair has provided quite a bit of theater to his overall appearance, it has also been a distraction. Now, with his hair short and wavy, even sticking up in parts, his face has come into relief. It's a damned fine face. Molded to his bones. I swear if I were to dig up his skull from his grave one hundred years from today, I would recognize it as his in an instant.

Will takes a step and the girls part like the Red Sea, eager to see exactly what he's going to do with his new-found manhood. I guess in my heart I always knew he would come to me first, but there was also that part of me that was scared he wouldn't. That his *hifi ulu* would ground him back in his life here, and away from the lives we've spent together.

"What do you think," he asks me.

"You look all right," I say. "You want to take a gander at yourself?"

"No. I think it's enough to see how you're looking at me."

Will reaches to the back of his head and pulls forward one last lock of his beribboned hair. I hadn't seen there was any left. He holds out his hand, and a pair of scissors are passed to him. Without a word, he offers them to me.

I look around, swallowing hard. So many stares, all expectant, like no one is sure what I'm going to do. Rose takes a deep breath, as if telling me to get on with it. Mr. Tongahai leans up onto his toes. My mum shrugs, rather bewildered. Everyone else is a blur, except for Will, of course. My hand is shaking, but I take the scissors and open them up. I can't help but to rub his hair between my fingers. Soft and thick, it was such a beautiful mane, and I feel a quick rush of sadness at its loss.

"Guess there's no turning back now," I say.

Will, in the eyes of his Niuean community, becomes a man in one last snip of steel against steel. I close my hand over the tress and the urge to burst into a good, hard cry subsides.

"Somehow, Will," Dr. Neville says. "You manage to look even more Niuean now than you did with the long hair."

He's got a point. Since most of the golden honey-hues, all kissed by the sun, have been clipped from his hair, what's left are the much darker roots. If you didn't know Rose and the parts of her imprinted on Will's features—the sharp-boned nose and defined chin—you'd think he was all islander.

Will puts his arm around me and opens himself up to the gathering. Rose stands next to her husband and folds her hands in front of her. She looks proud and happy. Even Mr. Tongahai is struggling to keep his emotions from spilling all over his face. "Welcome everyone," Will says. "Friends, family, our *magafaoa*. My parent's home has always been yours. The food on our table has been for us to share. And it will again be yours and your children's, even after it becomes mine and Angelie's."

There's a long beat of silence in the room. I toss a look over to Mum, and she and Aunt Kitty are backed up against the wall, each a mirror image of the other. Mouths open, eyes frozen in a look of surprise. In that moment, I realize I'm making the exact same face.

Will looks down at me and smiles. It feels as if Will and I are going to fall straight into each other's eyes and never come back. I want to kiss him very badly, but that won't do with all the people here, even if the Niueans aren't as prim as us mainlanders.

"Let's feast!" Rose calls out, snapping me and Will out of our trance. Everyone begins to clap, including the Vakaafis, and this puts the party at ease.

"It's all right," Ku mouths to me.

Will plants a kiss on top of my head.

I glance about the room and it does seem as if a weight has been lifted. I'm sure as word was going around about me and Will, there were more than a few raised eyebrows about how this night would play. Niueans are pretty hands off in their children's romantic choices from what I've seen, but they can be awfully clannish when they try. And, while someone like Rose was taken into the community without question, she's also grown up here. There's even a street named after her family—the Ogdens. I'm new and untested. For all they know, island life might not suit me at all and I'll end up breaking Will's heart, or worse, taking him away from here.

As Will and I smile and nod at the guests—our guests now, our guests in our future home—I notice one person is missing, gone and left the party altogether.

Oliana.

Chapter 16

THERE ARE ALL SORTS of fresh and delicious things the Tongahais have offered up for us to gorge on, and the lot of us stand near and around the bonfire enjoying them. I ignore most of the goodies in place of two full cans of Prince's corned beef hash.

"There's plenty where that came from, you know," Will tells me. "My mum always keeps a stash."

I elbow Will in the ribs.

"I'm just saying it's not the last time you'll ever have it. Niue may be off the beaten path, but we do get some mainland staples from the cargo ship. Vegemite and things."

I lean in and kiss Will right on the line of his jaw. "I hate Vegemite and I don't care about mainland fair. Not much anyway. I just want to be with you."

Will bends down and kisses me outright on the lips in front of everyone. It's not a scandal or anything. Not on Niue. I'm sure I'm the only one who gets a bit red in the cheek.

"Do you know where Oliana went?"

Will shakes his head. "Home, I guess. We had a long talk."

"Before the *hifi ulu*?"

"A couple of days ago, actually."

I feel a little sick hearing that, given what Will and I have been doing with our days.

"Is she all right?"

"She will be," Will says. "Not like other boys on the island aren't happy to see she's available."

I want to say, *you're not like other boys*, but I don't.

I glance over at the Vakaafis, who seem content in a conversation with Dr. Neville and Mr. Tongahai. They haven't looked at me all that much throughout the party, but they haven't been rude either. Not sure I would be as understanding in their place.

"Hiya," says Ku.

He's eating a fruit bat all roasted and dipped in a sticky sauce. Gives me the willies.

"Congratulations, Will. You finally made it. I, myself, had my hair cut when I was twelve, but we all grow to men at our own pace, my mum says."

"Some, not at all," Will razzes him. "Hair or no."

Ku laughs, mouth full of bat.

"So, you're making it official, the two of you. Looks like you're going to be one of us now," Ku says to me. "Makes the island all the better as far as I'm concerned."

"You may be the only one outside of Will who feels that way," I tell him.

Will puts his arm around me and Ku gives me some cheek.

"Aw, come on. You can't blame Oliana. As for our mum and dad, they're all right. My dad chose mum over Mary, our post mistress. She's part of our *magafaoa*, too, and was all done in about it until she married Albert Kai. Now she and mum go bathing together."

Somehow I can't imagine ever feeling warm enough

to go bathing with Oliana. I think at this point I'd rather swim with that shark who tried to eat me.

Mum shoots a glance my way. She and Aunt Kitty have been in a dither together, talking all tight-lipped and with their hands. Obviously about me, which is why I've avoided them. I guess I can't go on doing that forever.

"Will you two excuse me for a few minutes," I say, and Will and Ku take that as an opportunity to snag a couple more coldies.

Mum squares her shoulders when she sees me coming, and Aunt Kitty gets that *well, it's about time* look on her face.

"Good party," I say. "Interesting ritual."

Mum narrows her eyes at me.

"Angelie, Will is a wonderful bloke, but you've barely known him a month."

Mum's always one for getting right to the point.

"You've hated it here since we arrived and have only begun to tolerate it now that you've started running around with a beau."

"It just took a little while for me to settle in," I tell her. "You said it yourself. We're in a beautiful place, far from the war. I thought you wanted me to like it here."

Mum takes a hard pull on her coldie and wipes her mouth with the back of her hand. "I know you'll be eighteen this year, but don't you want to wait a bit? Court for a while."

She has no idea just how long Will and I have been courting.

"If it helps," I tell her. "I knew from the moment I saw him. And he knew, too. It's like we've known each other for thousands of years."

Aunt Kitty presses her lips together and blinks her eyes like a doe. "I think it's romantic," she says, about knocking me over with a feather.

"Kitty!" Mum cries.

"Can't help it," Kitty moons. "It's just like *Savage Lover*."

"It's nothing like *Savage Lover*, Kitty, and please leave your dime store novels out of this."

Aunt Kitty and I meet eyes and I bite my lip, looking down at my feet. We read *Savage Lover* together on the boat to Savage Island, and it was such fun. All about a girl from some place in America I've never heard of, who falls for a Hawaiian bloke on a mission trip. It's set back in the eighteen fifties and has lots of passionate gazes and frolics about the beach. The girl even ends up surfing and doing hula dances with the natives. Right scandalous, according to Mum.

"I promise never to do the hula," I say, and Aunt Kitty and I bust up.

Mum seals her lips closed, but can't disguise that there's a smile behind them just dying to come out.

"You married Paul when you were eighteen," Kitty reminds her.

Mum takes a deep breath flooded with memories. "Yes, I did."

"And Will saved my life. You said so yourself."

"I did that, too."

The devil spoken of comes up behind me. I can feel his breath on the crown of my head.

"Will," Mum says. At least she's got a nice tone for him.

He's come armed with rum punches and some sweeties Rose must have got from England: Violet candies, foil wrapped toffies, licorice and jellies. He holds out the little tray and Aunt Kitty plucks three of her favorites from a

porcelain dish flecked with daisies. Then she up and kisses
Will's cheek, which actually makes him visibly blush.

He turns to my mum. "I didn't mean to pull a surprise
like that. About Angelie and me."

Mum looks like she wants to say something, but doesn't.
I know how much she likes Will, but it's all a lot for her to
take in, and it's not like we can tell her the truth.

"I talked to my mum and dad about it," he continues.
"But I really wasn't meaning to say anything until I'd talked
to you first. Definitely not at the *hifi ulu*. It just slipped
out."

Will looks to me now. "I hadn't even asked you about it
all, at least not officially."

"And what do you have to say to that?" Aunt Kitty prods.

Mum raises up her eyebrows.

"What?" I say.

Will chuckles a bit nervously, and Mum looks at him
with tenderness. I bet he reminds her of Jay.

"The bo-, I mean man, deserves an answer," Mum tells
me.

"To which question?"

Will and Kitty and Mum give me a look of utter frustra-
tion, but then Will steps forward and turns to face me. He
takes my hand, goes down onto one knee and I feel like
such an idiot.

"This is the way you mainlander girls expect things to
go, isn't it?"

My mouth drops open and I hurry up to close it so I
don't look a fool. I am so fearfully happy all of a sudden.
My eyes well up in tears.

"Will you marry me," Will says, and then mouths *again*.

"Yes, of course."

Comes out as barely a whisper, but when I say it Aunt

Kitty jumps up and throws her arms around mum. She's happy as I've ever seen her. Mum's a bit wet-eyed herself and sniffles.

"Always and forever," I say. "Every time you ask."

THERE'S NOTHING LIKE a gathering of drunk islanders after one of their favorite ceremonies. Endless toasts about manhood and Will abound, all meant to make him cringe. Stories about his youth that are at once funny and moving, filled with revealing tidbits. Like one, told by Albert, the postmistress's husband, about how Will vowed to run away from home—swimming to the mainland if he had to—after a dream he had regarding the Pyramids of Giza. He'd only seen a picture in one of Rose's encyclopedias, but was somehow able to make them up just as they are in the sand on Hio Beach. Every detail in place.

"He's always been an odd bloke," Ku says, holding up his punch and throwing me a wink. "Don't say I didn't warn you."

Will pulls me close and whispers that we should think about slipping out. It's getting late and Dr. Neville's already gone. He tells his parents we're going for a moonlight walk and I do the same.

"Don't be gone too long. You've got guests to say goodbye to—the both of you."

I guess that's the closest I'll get to a *welcome to the family* from Mr. Tongahai at present, but I'll take it.

"Be careful," Aunt Kitty says.

The note of hysteria in her voice comes from one little

comment Mr. Tongahai made, saying he doesn't like the wind that's come on.

"Yes, the arches, Aunt Kitty, I'll be sure to stay clear of them."

She blows me a kiss and I catch it.

THE WIND HAS PICKED UP, slowing me and Will down as we trudge through the groves and up to the plateau, where Drs. Neville and Vogel are hunched over their spy machine trying to make a transmission. There's a ton of static as it is, and the whistle of the wind this high up is making it difficult to understand anything coming or going.

"Ainsley!" Dr. Neville shouts.

Something resembling a man's voice comes over the line, but I can't make out a thing he's trying to say.

"Does it sound like him?" I ask Will. He shrugs, unsure.

Finally, Dr. Neville puts his lips right up to the mouthpiece. He says, "Will Tongahai" and "Sherin" as loudly and distinctly as he can.

"Say again." The garbled voice comes through this time.

At the next break in the wind, Dr. Neville repeats the names. There's silence on the other end—not even an attempt at communication. We all sit around the transmitter for several minutes, staring at it, willing it to start talking to us again.

When it grumbles at last, I jump a bit.

"What was that he said?"

Neville cocks his head and Will leans in closer. Max Vogel stands, arms crossed.

"Prince George," Max says.

Neville looks up at him. "Are you sure?"

The transmitter sputters again, and this time it's quite clear. Whoever's on the line said, "Prince George."

"What on earth does he mean by that?" Will asks.

Dr. Neville takes a long, deep breath.

"It means he's coming. Harry Ainsley is coming ashore."

Chapter 17

THE DRIVE TO HIKUTAVAKE doesn't take long, but once there, we have to walk a good thirty minutes along a tropical forest trail past the tops of the Arches of Talava. We climb down and reach the coast and, from there, we can see a tiny, blinking light coming from a small boat that's cast off from Harry's submarine. Max Vogel takes out a pair of binoculars and looks out. The scene is strangely reminiscent of when Neville and Vogel arrived, only, as the boat gets closer, there's only one person in it. A slender bloke, from what I can see, in the white light of the moon. Will takes the binoculars from Max and looks close.

"It's definitely Harry," he says.

The boat's not much of a thing—couldn't hold more than a couple of men and a box of provisions. Must be the type used for clandestine jaunts like this one. The whole idea is terribly exciting and strange.

Harry Ainsley stumbles out of the boat, tripping over a lump of coral on the shallow bottom. It doesn't stop him from standing up, soaking wet, and taking hulking, splashing steps toward us. He's got skin pale as marble and dark hair in the way of the black Irish. Even in this light, I can tell his eyes are a crystal blue, like an arctic sky.

"Will!" he calls out.

He stops a good many steps away yet and puts his hands on his hips, breathing hard.

"What the bloody hell are you doing here, Harry?"

I've never heard Will curse before.

"It's good to see you, Will," Harry says.

Will looks a bit torn. I mean yes, he's happy to see Harry and wants to know what this is all about, but the fact remains that Harry Ainsley, his so-called best friend, ratted him out about joining the Navy.

I think Harry can see the dilemma written on Will's face and takes the few remaining steps forward.

"We've got a lot to talk about, mate," Will says.

"That we do."

Harry looks over at the scientists. "Dr. Neville and Dr. Vogel, I presume."

"You presume right," Dr. Neville says. "It's good to put a face to a voice, Harry."

Harry smiles. It's the upright smile of a well-raised son from a good family.

"I'm Angelie."

Harry glances over at me and gives a nod, but his attention is all on Will.

"I imagine we haven't got much time," Neville says over a loud blast of wind. "There must be a good place nearby where we can talk—maybe one of the caves?"

Will leads the way to a yawning hollow only a short break from where we beach Harry's boat. It's a grotto nicknamed the empty belly; a wet cave, it reflects the beam from our flashlight in the low water that covers its floor. But the coral is smooth and even furry with moss at parts, so I'm able to take off my sandals and carry them. Mum would go bloody crook if I wrecked a good pair.

There's a swell of rock towards the back, which provides a good place for us to climb on and sit, keeping dry.

"I almost didn't recognize you out there," Harry says. "Your hair."

"Will had his *hifi ulu* tonight," I explain.

"I see," Harry says, though I don't think he does.

"My hair cutting ceremony," Will clarifies, and Harry lights up, seeming to remember such a thing exists in Will's world.

"Blasted, Will," Harry says. "When my sub came to Niue . . . I guess I always knew I was meant to see you again."

"We were meant to join the Navy together."

Harry Ainsley looks down and shakes his head.

"Say something," Will says.

Harry tips his head up and meets Will's eyes. He's no coward, I can see that.

"I don't have anything to say, except that I couldn't let you go."

"Why?"

Harry runs his fingers through his short black hair.

"It was something you once said. I-I mean in your sleep. About a man with eyes like yours, only different in color."

"Another Nin'ti?" I say, and Harry looks at me, eyes wide. He picks up Neville's flashlight and shines it at my face. I hold out my hand to block some of its light stream, but still allow Harry a good hard look.

"My Lord," he says. "You're one of them, too."

He glances over at Neville and Vogel, and Neville shakes his head. "Not us, no," he tells him. "But I think you already knew about Will."

Harry nods.

"How?" Will asks him. "When I didn't even know."

Harry looks up at the cave ceiling as if beseeching God.

"I still can't believe it. Sometimes it all seems like some delusion, but then, here we are."

Harry puts his knees up, resting his arms on them. For a moment he looks like the boy he must have been when Will met him. Wasn't that long ago, but from the look of Harry, it might as well have been a decade.

"From the beginning you were talking in your sleep," Harry says. "I'm used to talking and snoring, even sleep-walking. I've been away at school since I was a young lad of six. Only your talk wasn't the odd sentence or word blurted out. You would actually sit up and have entire conversations with me. And when you did, it was like you were a completely different person."

"What do you mean?"

"I mean you didn't even look like yourself. Your whole demeanor changed, the tone of your voice and manner of your speech. Yet you were totally lucid. Not some raving maniac or anything."

I think about Will's transformation when he held the ancient statue and shiver.

"At first you talked of the past, and with such specificity. Wars and crusades. People you'd known. Sometimes things so obscure. I started going to the library to verify what I could of the stories you were telling me."

"And what did you find?" I ask him.

"That Will was either an expert on the minutiae of history . . ."

"Or he *was* history," Neville says.

"During the day, you became obsessed with your dreams and having them tattooed on your body. It was all so bloody insane that I didn't know what to do at first."

"Why didn't you tell me?"

"Why? Because you—the other you—asked me not to, that's why. He . . . he's my friend, too. Maybe even a closer friend to me than you, Will."

"What's his name?" I ask.

Harry takes a deep breath and blinks his eyes.

"Nif. His name is Nif."

"And did Nif ever mention me?"

Harry looks surprised at my question at first, but then a look of realization dawns on his face.

"Sherin?"

I nod.

"Of course," he says, all wonderstruck. "The green eyes. They are like nothing I've ever seen. Nif always said they were the color of an enchanted stone and he was right. But he also told me everything else about you. Your long hair, as rich as the soil, and skin like tanned suede without so much as a fleck or mole. And you, you're so fair and have all these freckles. I guess it's easy to be deceived by appearances."

He can't stop staring at me, and it's not as if I can blame him, but I do feel awfully self-conscious about it. I touch Will's arm and realize that the girl painted on it—with the long, dark hair—is the one Harry is speaking of.

"He talked of your courage, too, and so many other things." Harry flits his eyes over at Will, then back to me. "You're the reason, you know."

"I don't understand."

"You're why I couldn't let Will join the war. I was afraid, if he did, he wouldn't find you."

"Harry," Will says. "When I was . . . dreaming . . . I told Sherin you had a message for her. Is that true?"

Harry folds his hands on top of his knees and shrugs. "Only that you're looking for her."

"That's all?" Neville asks.

"You were desperate to find her," Harry tells us. "Because you loved her, but also because you said it was of the utmost importance. Even more important than the war."

"And you believed all this?"

Harry leans in, placing his hand on Will's forearm. "Oh, yes. I would trust Nif with my life."

"But not me?"

Harry smiles. "You, too, Will. It's just different. Nif needed me to help you. And Nif, well, he's already a warrior, you see. And has been in so many lives throughout the centuries. I figured we could take his advice, as he knew much more than the both of us." Harry's eyes drift away to the mouth of the cave. "There have been so many times in these months when I wished he was with me. To give me guidance. War's a terrible thing."

"You regret joining up?" Will asks him.

Harry turns his head sharply. "Never."

"Gentlemen, and Angelie," Dr. Neville says. "This brings us to another critical subject at hand. Have you had any luck with our more immediate pursuits since our last transmission, Harry?"

Harry nods slow and sure.

"The Yanks have been going after the Jap subs and done significant damage to their fleet. We've been given a wide berth to sink as many Japanese ships as we can, you see. It's not always good news. Last week we sank a Hell Ship. That's a transport carrying Allied POWs and Romusha slave laborers. It was a mistake. We didn't mean to. All those poor Yanks, just gone."

Harry takes his head in his hands. It's all he can do to keep from falling apart.

Dr. Neville puts his hand on Harry's shoulder. "But *Akuma* remains at large."

"Slippery bastard," Harry says. "Sorry, keep forgetting there's a lady present."

"Max and I think we may have something for you."

Harry looks up. He lets his hands down from his head, leaving his hair sticking up like Tintin's.

"We know *Akuma* has been skulking around Oceana for some time, and have assumed she's staying close to Nuie to keep from being detected, obviously, but also to remain available to give support in the ongoing clashes over the Solomon Islands."

"You don't think that's what they're doing?"

"Maybe, maybe not. But if I were the Japanese and had a stealth ship like *Akuma*, one hugely successful at sneak attacks, I might think about sending her to Tongatapu, the Allied staging point for shipping in these parts."

Harry takes in a deep breath through his nose. Sucks on his teeth a bit, thinking.

"A lot more action in the Solomons. What with Bougainville."

"Exactly. Why lurk around here? Unless, of course, you're planning a strike that's close by, relatively speaking. Tonga is less than half the distance away than the Solomon Islands." Dr. Neville goes forearms to knees again. "Max and I think we intercepted a transmission—possibly from *Akuma* and definitely Japanese."

"When?"

"Yesterday. We were able to record part of it."

"I'd like to have a listen to that."

Neville raises a brow. "You speak Jap?"

"A few words," Harry says. "Maybe enough to get an

idea. We can always reach out to Saito, a Yank on board the *U.S.S. Nautilus*. He's from Hawaii and speaks fluent Japanese."

We'd left the spy machine nestled in some dry grass a few minutes hike up from the beach. Didn't want to risk it getting wet. Neville suggests we all go back to have a listen.

"You can just give me the reels," Harry tells us. "I've got a waterproof pouch we can put them in and I'll take them back to the boat. We'll want to comb through everything, from background noise to possible codes they might be speaking. These things aren't always so straightforward."

We make our way out of the cave and up to the trail, the lot of us. There, the wind blows into the tops of the trees, making them bow and sway. Harry seems to enjoy being on land and strokes the leaves of the ferns as we go by. Reminds me of how I used to follow my brother through the gangway behind our house. The way he used to run his hands along the bushes and whistle. That one carefree glimpse, from another life it seems, feels like a warm bath. That is until I roll my ankle again. Squatting down, I grip it tight and bite my lip. Damn it hurts, worse than before as it's already tender from the other times I've done it.

"Idiot," I say. Serves me right for not watching where I'm going.

"You're not so bad as that." Will crouches next to me and takes my ankle gently into his hands. He shines the flashlight on it, and I can see how it's already pink and starting to swell up. "Go ahead, all of you. I'll stay with Angelie."

"What? And leave the doctors to stumble through the jungle in the dead of night?"

"We'll be all right," Neville says.

"I'm sure you will. But it'll take you twice as long if you

take a wrong turn at the twisted root that looks like every other twisted root to everyone but Will."

"Angelie," Will starts.

"You know it's true. And I'll be right fine with just the moon for company, if you can get me out of the brush before you go. A little wind will feel nice on my ankle to tell you the truth."

"I'll stay with her," Harry says. "I pulled a muscle in my leg a few days back and wasn't looking forward to a trek over slippery roots and such."

Will bends toward me and kisses my nose. For a moment there I wish that everyone would disappear and he could kiss me again. Longer, and on the lips, among other places. I can see Will thinks the same.

"It'll be okay, Will," Harry says. "I'll get her out of the brush and we'll wait for you by the arches."

Our resident scientists look impatient to go and Will helps me up, careful I don't put any weight onto by foot. I take his hand and open his palm, kissing it there. Don't know what makes me do that. Without a word, Will takes my hand and does the same.

"You'll be back in sight of fifteen minutes, maybe less, knowing you."

Will nods, kissing my temple this time. I'm aware of the wet imprint of his lips as a bit of the breeze comes through the heavy curtain of greenery.

"It's hardly a long time," I tell him. "I wouldn't get my hair in curlers about it. Not that you have much hair left."

Damn I love his smile.

Watching them go, I can't help but feel a strange loneliness. One that hits me with a sharp stab when Will turns around one more time and mouths, "I do love you," before disappearing into the wild tangle of leaves and vines.

Harry goes to pick me up, but I suggest he lets me hop on his back instead. "Given your leg injury," I say.

Harry sniffs a bit and turns around. He's a good bloke.

"You never pulled a muscle, did you?"

Harry shakes his head. "I was trying to find a way to get you alone, and then you rolled that ankle of yours."

"Wish I could say it was part of my grand plan," I tell him. "So, the message from Nif. It wasn't what you said."

"Well, he did say that. It's just that it wasn't the only thing Nif said."

I climb onto Harry's back. He's lean, and smaller boned than Ku or Will, but strong nonetheless. Doesn't seem to have a bit of a problem holding me up as we start to go.

"Will isn't supposed to know? I mean, Nif doesn't want him to know whatever this message is."

"He told me whatever Will knows is up to you to tell him."

I think on that for a bit, and it does seem like such a big responsibility. I mean in the long scheme of things, the one that's run over thousands of years. It occurs to me how nice it would be to have someone like Harry in my life. A friend who can talk to the other me . . . this Sherin. Get some answers.

"It's about the other Nin'ti, isn't it," I say to Harry. "The one Nif talked about while Will was dreaming."

Harry nods.

"Have you met him?"

"No, God no. It's only what Nif told me, and that was enough of a horror."

Harry stops under a canopy of vines that opens out onto the Arches of Talava. The moon floats above the ocean like a woman's profile done in ivory on a cameo pin. Such a lovely thing. He puts me down carefully, helping me land on one foot, and eases me onto a comfortable tuft of grass on the ground. I can hear the powerful gusts of wind that come up like waves over these natural bridges. The sea below us is loud and rough, stirred up by the restlessness of the air. It's good to be under the shelter of the foliage.

"He's here to protect you, you know," Harry says. "Nif, I mean. And Will. Sometimes Nif also needs to protect Will from himself. He's damned arrogant, if you'll excuse me saying so."

"It's all right. Damn is actually my favorite word ever. And you're right, Will is damned arrogant."

Harry laughs and glances my way. He seems at once drawn in by my eyes and uncomfortable about them. I guess I would be in his place too.

"Nif said that in some ways things were easier in the past," he goes on to tell me. "A boy saw a lot before he became a man, then. Death, war. People being sliced and burned. We learn things much later today. Many never see such things at all, unless there's a war."

Not for the first time, I wonder what Harry has seen since joining the Navy.

"Is that why Nif is keeping things from Will? Because Will isn't ready?"

Harry shrugs. "He wouldn't say."

"But I am ready? For whatever you're going to tell me, I mean."

Harry's eyes become moist and focused. He tenses his lips and shakes his head.

"No one can ever be ready for what I have to tell you." Harry folds his hands, squeezing them tight, as if in prayer. I fold mine, too. A little prayer can never hurt.

"I didn't think it would be so hard."

"To tell me?"

Harry nods. "Nif, he told me so much about you. Not just about your eyes and what you looked like when he first saw you. He told me of what's in your heart . . . and his. I guess I didn't mean to, but I started to love you, too."

He turns to me and does look right into my eyes this time. "I'd never!" He says. "I shouldn't have opened my mouth. It's just that with the war still raging on, I tend to say what's on my mind, just in case."

"It's all right," I tell him. "I know you didn't mean it like that."

"I did," Harry says. "I meant it exactly like that. But still, I would never, you know. Nif is my friend. I'd do anything for him. So is Will." He gazes up at the moon. "And you. I'd do anything for you, too. I'm glad you and Will are safe here. Feels like the war is a million miles away on this rock and that nothing could touch you."

There's a sound come up behind us from the way we came. At first I think it's Will; that he might have come back, and I strain to see in the darkness. I can tell right straight that it can't be Will—this bloke is even thinner than Harry. And when he comes closer, I get a good whiff of him, which makes my blood run cold.

Evening in Paris.

Damn.

It's not a bloke at all. It's Oliana.

Chapter 18

HER EYES ARE DISTANT, like they were when she came to see me earlier today—or rather yesterday now. She's still wearing the dress she had on at the *hifi ulu*, and her hair is neat and garnished with flowers. She looks sad and pretty, like a girl in a Gauguin painting. Except for one thing. Oliana is holding a gun.

"Get up," she says.

Harry stands slowly, his hands palms up. "Just a minute here, Miss. Why don't you go ahead and hand the pistol to me? You don't want it going off on accident."

"I don't know who you are or why you're here," Oliana says to him. "But you can go. This has nothing to do with you."

"I'll only go if I can take her with me."

"Suit yourself then," she says. "Stay."

I pull myself up by the scaly trunk of a young palm, wobbling on my one good foot.

"Where did you get that?"

"Dr. Neville's place. He keeps it in a drawer under his shirts. I don't think he's touched it since he came here."

"Oliana," I say. "You don't even know how to work one of those. I know I don't."

"Doesn't look so hard. I have seen movies, you know."

Harry takes a step forward and Oliana points the pistol at him.

"Miss, I actually do know how to work a firearm, and I would feel much better if you'd give it to me before you end up doing something you'll regret."

"You don't know anything about me."

"But I do," Harry tells her. "You're Oliana. Will talked of you often at school. I was his roommate, you see. In England."

Harry's revelation does register on Oliana's face, but only some, like it's of vague interest.

"The way you'd swim together in the Namukulu, catching fish with your bare hands. And that one time a sea snake got tangled in your hair, but you had the temerity to help it unravel itself and set it free. He told me so much about you, it almost feels like we've met."

"That was a long time ago," Oliana says.

She indicates that we should move to the end of the canopy and onto the arches, where the wind is blowing in huffs and puffs.

Harry looks back to where Oliana wants us to go, and then around us at the thick walls of vegetation. I can see what he's thinking. We're in close quarters here, and if the gun goes off there's a good chance it will make a hit. Out there, we can put some space between us and her, and the wind will make it much harder for a novice to aim straight.

Harry takes my arm and drapes it over his shoulder, holding me up at the waist. "She's hurt, Oliana," he says. "We'll have to take it slowly."

Putting any weight on my ankle is blood agony right now, with a pain so sharp and achy at once that I have to catch my breath. Harry, I think, is buying time by not offering to carry me despite how much I'm struggling. The more Oliana can think about what she's doing, the more she might start wondering if this was such a fine idea.

Seems like it takes forever to get to the end of the canopy, and once we do step out onto the top of one of the natural bridges, a whistling gust of wind comes up nearly blowing Harry and me to our knees. It goes as quick as it came, leaving us standing in a gentle breeze.

Oliana looks me up and down, almost like she doesn't quite believe I exist, and that frightens me. It's easier to pull the trigger on a phantom.

"You can't want to kill me," I say. "What would it do to your life?"

"My life? What hasn't already been done to my life?"

Harry steals a glance my way and pulls me closer.

"No, Angelie. I'm not going to kill you." Oliana holds up her wrist and takes a deep sniff of Evening in Paris. "I'm going to kill myself. I just want you to see it."

"What?"

"I'm not afraid you know. I was there when my grand-mother died and she had such a sweet smile. She said, 'Oh, goodness, will you look at that?' just before she slipped away."

"Oliana, you can't. That would just destroy your mum."

"She'll still have Ku, and our older brother in New Zealand. I'm sure he'll come back, and that'll make her happy."

"No, it won't!"

Oliana marches past us and out onto the middle of the arch, the pistol tight in her hand.

"What do you know?"

"I've watched my own mum mourn my father and my brother," I tell her. "Damn near tore her apart."

"She seems all right to me."

She cuddles the gun close to her chest like a dolly and tip-toes out to the edge of the arch. There, she looks down onto the sharp bits of coral that break the surface just as the water recedes. I know something of the siren of suicide. I mean, I've never wanted to kill myself, but I have seen the way grief can feel like such a dead end. And I realize it's possible I actually have killed myself in a previous life or lives, so maybe I have a better idea of self-murder than I think. All I can say is that I do understand why such a dramatic end is appealing. It doesn't just promise to stop the pain, but transform it. Give it a whole other story, one that you can control instead of one that's been hoisted upon you. It's all a lie, of course, but it's the sort of lie you want to believe. Like convincing yourself people don't like you only because they're jealous.

"You're a demon," she spits at me, her teeth gritted. "You hypnotized him! And my brother and those scientists, too—even my parents say to me that I should accept Will's choice."

"I'm not a demon, or anything like that. And I can't help it about Will. We love each other, that's all. I know how awful that is to hear and I don't want to hurt you, but it's true. It's love, Oliana. Magical in its own right, but not black magic."

Despite the odd circumstances surrounding Will's and my relationship, I know this to be true. Whatever it is between Will and me, it's good. From its very core, it's right. And even in this moment, with Oliana in so much pain and ready to do herself harm, I would never give it up. What Will and I have is bigger than this, bigger than mothers and fathers and dreams, bigger than any one life.

"It is black magic," she says. "Look what it's done to me."

Without as much as a whisper of warning, Harry let's go of me and I teeter on my one good foot, just managing to stay upright. He rushes Oliana, who barely has a chance to let her mouth gape open when he knocks the gun out of her hand. It flies over the edge into the reef and, to my horror, she moves to take one big step out to follow its doomed path.

"Oliana!"

Will's voice comes up from behind me and I have never been so happy to hear a sound in my life. Oliana stops and turns in his direction, looking right past me. She's so close to the precipice that I fear a deep breath could blow her over.

"You once told me a full moon inspires lunacy," Will says. "I didn't think you were serious."

"Is that what it did to *you*?" Oliana says. "There was a full moon the night you met her."

Will brushes past me, his finger touching the center of my palm with a quick and furtive stroke as he goes by. He heeds the warning in Oliana's eyes and doesn't come too close. He stops just on the other side of Harry, a good three long strides from the edge she's practically dangling over.

"Whatever you do, please don't tell me how you never wanted to hurt me. At least spare me that."

"I won't say it," Will says softly. "What I will say is that I'm thinking I never knew you at all. Maybe you didn't know me either."

"What are you talking about? I've known you all my life. We were born three days apart! There was hardly a day we didn't spend together until you went off to school."

Will takes a small step forward and Oliana doesn't move. Emboldened, he tries one more, but that one is a no-go. Oliana puts out her hand for him to stop.

"When you left, I was so afraid you'd never come back," Oliana continues. "You never seemed like you were from here. Not even as a boy. I wondered if maybe it was because your mother is British, but in a way, she's more an islander than you are."

"I can't help what I am," Will says.

There's a rustle under the canopy again and I know it must be the Drs. Neville and Vogel, come back with their spy machine. They stay a few paces behind me, wary of making any sudden moves or causing Oliana to do the same.

Harry has no such compunction. He lunges at Oliana, grabbing her arm, but she spins right around, boxing him on the side of the head. It knocks him off balance, and he stumbles backward and falls flat on his back. I hear his head hit the rock surface of the bridge with a thud.

"Harry!" Will dives down and begins speaking to him in a low voice, trying to get a response. Harry lies there, eyes closed. I can't even tell if he's breathing. Dr. Neville goes to our injured friend, crouching at his side and searching for a pulse. It appears he's got one, thank God. I limp over, too, none at all caring that it bloody hurts just to move now. My ankle's puffed up like a blowfish.

Oliana is breathing hard. "I didn't mean to!"

I can see Harry's bleeding quite a lot. His blood is all over Will's hands and looks black as motor oil in the moon glow. I reach under my dress to my slip and begin ripping off strips for Dr. Neville to use as a bandage. Dr. Vogel takes them from my hand.

I hear Harry groan and I flush with relief. I even hear him say my name. I figure if he can form words he's probably going to be okay. Dr. Neville voices a similar opinion.

"Oh, thank God," Oliana says.

A bit of a howl comes through the air. The wind is picking up again, swinging my hair all over. I go to hop my way over to Harry, but just then a big gust hits, making me step back hard onto my bum ankle. I curse and teeter just as another blast swings in, actually picking me up off the arch. Will looks over his shoulder, and a cold horror comes over him. He jumps up and away from Harry, his arm drawn like a sword. For a moment there, our fingers are but a hair apart.

Everything slows down and I seem to float for a bit, looking down onto the surface of the arch. I see them all and they me. Dr. Neville, Dr. Vogel, Harry, Oliana and Will. I'm too far. I know it as well as they do. Even if I can manage to touch the side as I land, I'll just slide down the rock and end up in the reef anyway. Just like Dr. Neville's gun. It's funny what goes through your mind at a time like this. I think of the first time Will kissed me—on the beach under these very arches. The joy with which he held my face, bringing it so close it was as if we'd come together to form the dark and light side of the moon. I think of the softness of his lips and the cool wetness of his tongue. The way his long hair had felt in my fingers. As I begin to fall, and yet another rough wind blows me even further out, I think, "Damn, Aunt Kitty was right."

Chapter 19

I T'S NOT HARD to see why ghosts are said to moan and rattle their chains.

We cannot touch the living; those we loved with our beating hearts and whose memories we carefully place in our souls, curating a menagerie of losses.

The mother who loved me, her twin sister, Kitty. On the night before my funeral I visit them each in their dreams. I thank them for loving me and wish I could leave them with more than two broken hearts.

But it's Will who needs me more than anyone. Even if he's the only one assured of seeing me again.

"This isn't the end," Kandi Neville says to him. "You know that."

Will hasn't spoken a word since my body crashed onto the coral rocks beneath the Arches of Talava. Not because he can't. Words speak of futures and he feels he has none to speak of. Not on Niue.

Tonight he lies in bed wide awake, as he has every night since my death. Desperate for a sleep that will not come. As the dawn breaks, he gets up before anyone else. There's a heavy slumber that's hit the Tongahai household. The hard labor of sorrow has exhausted them, and Rose didn't even notice that her Kadupul flower had bloomed and withered the night before.

He dresses in the same cut-off pants and undershirt he peeled off when he first showed me the stories of our lives together; the ones he'd been dreaming about in Canterbury and tattooed onto nearly all of his flesh. He walks out into his yard, where the bonfire had been lit and the pig had turned on a spit. Where the story of the Nin'ti was told by Cornelius Kandinsky Neville. Will misses Harry, who has gone back to his submarine, and hunting *Akuma*. Harry is one of the few people who truly understands.

"I'll come see you after the war is finished, I promise," Harry told him. "There's a great deal we need to talk about. You and me and Nif."

Will nodded vaguely.

He's no longer thinking about Harry when he hikes up the path to Avaiki cavern, though. His lips move as he repeats to himself our every conversation, as if he's trying to decipher a code.

From the ledge, he dives into the clean aquamarine waters and backstrokes about the pool. Will floats on his back, staring up at the twinkling rock crystals that stud the cave ceiling. After a while, he climbs out of the pool and lies down on our mossy coral bed. He folds his hands over his chest and closes his eyes. Sleep comes easily this time.

There is a wind in the desert that speaks of secrets.

Nif's soul, as warm and red as a gush of fresh blood fills the cavern.

I love when you sing that song to me, The Songs of the Desert Wind.

It was a song we knew long ago, when we first met. A song that spoke of a time when people were not yet too secure in their comforts to imagine a world of mystery.

I'll miss the freckles across your nose; and the ones splattered over your shoulders and spilling down your back. The soft pillow of flesh beneath your thumb, and how your hands moved over my body with such a sense of yen. All of the ways I could see a new facet of your soul through the shapes and colors of another body.

Our time was too short.

A school of silvery fish stir in the pool. They follow in a circle, swimming faster, until they are whirling like a cyclone. The cavern glows, lighting up every form of rock, disturbing the bats. They extrude from the cave in a fury.

This is how souls make love. It is a charge of electricity and surge of energy that can turn this cavern into a pile of rubble, or remake it. Sharpen its crystals, twist its rock pillars and make its waters restless.

Sherin, I think we've kept too many secrets from each other.

He's right, but I don't know how to even begin to tell him mine. Some things are best locked away.

The sea rushes into the cavern, rising up and over Will's sleeping body. At first I lose sight of him, but then the water calms. He twitches. I want him to open his mouth and take the water into his lungs, just as he meant to do. Let the ocean take him out with the high tide and bring him to me for more than a dream. We could wait together until we're born again. Maybe then, we could tell each other all of our secrets.

But Will thrashes under the water.

He shakes his head like a dog, and looks around as if he's surprised to find himself here. Sitting up on a higher point of the coral bed, he watches the water rise around him. His eyes move all over the cavern in a desperate search.

"Sherin!" It's the first time he's used his voice in some days and it's raspy.

Stay. Die here. You've had many worse deaths than drowning. That's the devil in me talking. For a Nin'ti, suicide is a disruption of our journey; makes it harder to find one another in our next life.

Go. Go home.

⊙

THE TIDE IS TOO HIGH now to go back the way he came, and Will swims out of Avaiki. Instead of going over the rock reef and wading up to shore, he swims right to the hot-orange coral. A couple of yards from its edge, where the water is too shallow to swim anymore, he stands up and walks the rest of the way out of the sea, slicing his feet to ribbons again. Continuing into the village, he doesn't go to the Vakaafis house as he did when I was injured and he was carrying me. There's a puff of smoke coming from out of their kitchen window, but he doesn't even glance that way. Will tracks his bloody footprints across the smoothed stone paths, trailing around an unruly mango tree, heavy with fruit.

Behind it is the modern guest cottage reserved for esteemed visitors to this island. Far less charming than the thatched roof homes the regular folk live in, it's made of cinder blocks and has a tin roof. But it does have amenities like consistent hot water and a working refrigerator. The only nicer place is the Tongahais'. Will beats on the door and Dr. Cornelius Kandinsky Neville answers, his face full of concern for the young man he's grown to care for.

"I must go with you," Will says.

Chapter 20

THE LIVING WORLD loses its crisp edges and becomes a blur of shapes and colors. A mess of voices. This always happens as I drift away from one life and wait for the next. But I hang on, as I always do, trying to catch the clear glimpses that flash before me on occasion. Most of the time, I just have to make out as best I can.

Not long after Harry's return to his submarine, the British Navy hunted down *Akuma* on her way to Tongatapu and blew her out of the water. Neville and Vogel had been right. And if there is a silver lining to my sudden end, of having to part with love so soon, it's that I got to watch *Akuma* die her own fiery death, pieces of her floating down to the ocean bottom.

"That's for you, Angelie," Harry said, as he stood on the starboard of his sub and watched the black smoke from the Japanese stealth ship boil and billow into the sky.

When Harry returned to Niue after the war as he'd promised, Will was gone. His family knew he was in North Africa somewhere with their scientist friends, and that he promised to pick up his mail in Cairo every month.

Haunting the desert, Will and the scientists use a miniature of the map room I showed them—one Max made with his meticulous hands and German precision. I catch a glimpse of Will here and there, wrapped in the robes of a desert wanderer, just as he was in our first life, when he was called Nif.

I see Will in Cairo some years after that, but the earth is too distant for me to make out any details. But one day, Will goes into Neville's hotel room after having bribed a clever young boy to steal the key from behind the front desk. He knows just what he's looking for and digs into the fancy leather tote where the archeologist keeps the ancient statue his father had bought from a trinket seller. The one Nif and I encountered in our first life together, and most recently on Savage Island. For the first time since we followed Neville and Vogel to Vaikona, Will takes the statue into his hand. It is then that he becomes clear to me again. His dark, wavy hair now falls past his shoulders. And he's grown a beard.

In an instant, his posture changes, his neck elongates, and his expression becomes one of authority and purpose. He tucks the statue into his jacket pocket and goes out into the streets of Cairo. He seems to know just where he's going, and enters the Darb al Ahmar district's maze of serpentine alleyways. It's good to see it again—all lined with medieval facades and punctuated by old mosques that ring the call to prayer as only old mosques do. With hollow bells that call out to past centuries, beckoning them to keep the modern world at bay. Past the bustling chaos of the Gate of Bab Zuweila, he turns down a narrow path that dead ends at the modest home of an apothecary. But as he raises his hand to knock, he's assaulted from behind by a rather tall man as far as men from these parts go. His assailant raises a curved blade high into the air and plunges it into my love's body over and over again. Before losing consciousness, Nif looks up into the man's face and narrows his eyes in recognition.

"*Ka' pahr ha t'on,*" he says, in the tongue of the Rah'a. *You only give me back to her.*

"No," says the man in English. "Not this time. I only leave you to suffer, as I have."

AS MY NEW LIFE BECKONS, the living world comes into relief again. The sharp coral edges of the place I briefly called home take shape, and it's as if the whole island is alive with our fate, mine and Nif's. As if it always has been.

Will is near on thirty now. He's just returned to Niue after a long and painful convalescence. I see him walk through his orchard with a heavy limp. He's deep in thought and goes all about the island to the places we used to go. Even if long walks now cause him a great deal of pain.

He sits on the plank after the sun has set, and remembers the night he asked me to meet him there. After Ku and I had gone, he sat alone on the plank and prayed that I could be happy living with him on Savage Island.

You know I could be happy living with you anywhere, I tell him on his first night home, after he's drifted off into his dreams.

I know, he says. *And Niue isn't a hardship. It may be the most beautiful place we've ever lived together.*

Will begins to stir.

Nif, what happened in that alleyway in Cairo? Why did you take that statue with you?

He doesn't answer, as Will wakes up right then and Nif returns to his body. He gets out of bed in order to move about to ease the ache in his back and leg. Chronic pain makes it difficult for him to sleep through the night.

In the morning, Oliana comes by. She lost a child she made with her second cousin from Aofi, and she and the father have separated. He moved to New Zealand last year, she tells him.

"I don't miss him," she says. "I never loved him at all."

That night, Will lets her stay. And the night after that, and from there on out. I want to know more about Cairo, but I can't go to him at night anymore. Not when their every kiss is like a bath of acid for me.

But I understand. I do understand. Will needs someone and Oliana loves him.

"Is that a letter from Dr. Neville," she asks him as she sets herself to make tea. It's bright and early on Christmas Eve, and she lights the new stove in the Tongahai's kitchen.

Will nods. He tells her that the Drs. Neville and Vogel are back at the University of Chicago. Dr. Neville has a new son. He has not told her about their failed attempts at finding the lost city of the Rah'a. Or the necklace they'd found in the desert. An amulet with a bloodstone, and two interlinked circles with a star in the center. He never talks about the attack on him and claims to remember nothing before or right after.

"We should send him a gift. What did they name the boy?"

"Cornelius Klimt Neville."

"How nice," she says. "Is Klimt a family name?"

"Something like that."

He looks out onto the yard where they'll be building a bonfire tonight, and the *magafuoa* will be gathering round, feasting on pig and coconut crabs.

JUST AFTER THE NEW YEAR, Will goes to help his widowed father with repairing a fence for their goats. He lifts up his shirt and looks down at his scar from the alley in Cairo. It's raised and as red as if it were a fresh wound, but doesn't resemble at all the many deep gashes that had been inflicted upon him. Four in his leg alone, three to his side and another in his stomach. This scar, like the ones on his back from years ago, has changed. It has moved, becoming two interlinked circles with a star in the center, just like the amulet.

Will's not paying proper attention as he makes to pound a metal spike into a post of wood. He can't get the amulet out of his mind, and the hammer comes down all wrong. The spike makes a grisly tear of his arm, the one tattooed with images of fire.

"Damn," Will says, and he smiles, thinking of me.

Will wraps it up himself, not bothering with calling on the *taulaatua*. There's not much she can do that he can't manage himself. But over the next few days, he develops a terrible fever.

"It is a quiet march to death, but sure." The *taulaatua* knows it from the moment she sees him, and asks Oliana why she didn't call right away. She might have been able to help him.

"Angelie," Oliana says.

"What?"

"Nothing."

As the hours go by and Will worsens, Oliana waits for him to say that name. Angelie. But he just lies there, burning hot and still as a corpse.

"He'll be fine. I'll make sure of it," she tells Will's father.

Oliana runs back to the *taulaatua* and bursts in through her door, falling onto her knees.

"There's an *aitu* on the island," she cries. A punishing spirit who has tortured her—first with the attack on Will in Cairo and now with his blood infection.

"It's her, I know it," she says. "Angelie."

The *taulaatua* is skeptical, but goes with her to the Arches of Talava, so they can lift the *tapu* Oliana believes I have left upon Savage Island. Upon Will's very life and hers. They dance and light herbs, saying prayers both island-born and Christian. Oliana raises her hands to the heavens.

"It was my fault. Take me!"

But the sky doesn't change. It remains gray and overcast as it's been all day. The *taulaatua* tells her she doesn't think that's a good sign.

When Oliana returns home to the plantation, Will has not changed. I must say she is good to him, but I expected nothing less. She tends to him as I wish I could, all the while waiting for him to say it. My name. Angelie.

When he sleeps, she caresses his brow and tells him it's all going to be all right. The *tapu* is gone. Still, he grows sicker. His flesh hotter to the touch, his lips dry and cracking.

Will's father has gone for the pastor and Oliana comes very close to him, hovering over his face. She begs him to unburden his soul and say the name of the girl he'd loved. The girl who left him so young.

"I'll understand," she says. "Say it, please. Say Angelie."

Only as the hours go by, she becomes more anxious. The pastor has come and gone and Will's father is on his other side, humming a funeral song. Will lets out a moan, barely audible, and Oliana squeezes his hand. She begins to doubt herself and wonder if she can stand hearing the name. It has become as painful to her as the prospect of Will's death. As my helplessness is to me.

As Will takes his dying breath, his eyes fluttering, rolling back, his lips parting, she knows the time has come and she steels herself to hear it.

"God help me," she says.

Will's voice, in a chirr, begins the whisper she's been waiting for.

But Angelie is not what she hears.

"What?" she says, bringing her ear to his lips. "Tell me."

Then, from the very bottom of his very last breath, Will says, "Sherin," leaving her in a state of befuddlement.

FROM NEARLY the moment of his death, Nif feels the urge to be born just as I do.

But in the meantime, however brief, we are *here*.

Here there is no night sky. We are the night sky. We can take the moon in our arms, shoot arrows with Sagittarius. Love with the power of a universe that is ever expanding.

Soon I'll have hands, and can touch you again.

A body has its own pleasures.

And a heart that flutters like an angel tern each time I see you.

That fire will be lit again. The fire of birth. Our ongoing quest. But until then, we have this.

THEIR STORY CONTINUES IN BREATH...

AVAILABLE EXCLUSIVELY ON AMAZON!

[BREATH]

Chapter 1

RARELY DO I GET more than a few glimpses of flesh and blood people when I'm still on the other side. A free soul and metaphysical whatchamacallit, if you will. Most of the time, when I try to look into the lives of friends and loved ones who are still among the living, it's as if I'm watching them through a piece of gauze. No real details, just shapes and fuzzy smears of color. I'm lucky to hear a few sentences from a conversation.

It's only before a rebirth that my vision into the living world becomes crystal clear. And it's thrilling. Like the movie trailer for a sequel you've been dying to see. I'm able to haunt places I've been to, people still tied to my destiny, who I might see again. Even things. Like an old, little statue.

A bird's head.

A lion's mouth.

Once-red wings, still flecked with the faint remnants of paint in some areas, but mostly worn to clay.

The body of a strong, thin man.

Clawed feet clutching a flower.

The man who holds this little statue is wearing a kef-fiyeh, of sorts. It's square and white, flowing down to his shoulders, and topped with a blue Chicago Cubs cap. The rest of him is all Indiana Jones. Rumpled cotton shirt

– probably white once, but now somewhere between beige and gray, with large, wet ovals around the armpits. Soft worn khakis held up by an oiled, leather belt that's genuinely old – his grandfather's, if I'm not mistaken. Only on his feet, instead of the weatherworn brown oxfords Indy would have worn, are a pair of Nike Air VaporMax Flyknit utility shoes. Black. He squints up at the sun, takes off his baseball cap and wipes his face, also black, with his makeshift keffiyeh.

"Dr. Neville!" The heavy doors to the Egyptian Museum of Antiquities groan open, and a young man, barely five feet tall and sporting the most outrageous curly, chestnut hair, scampers over to him.

"Not another bomb threat," Neville says, wearily pocketing the statue.

"No, no," the young man insists.

Neville laments that his lecture at the museum has already been postponed twice.

"It's still on, I think," the young man tells him. "But, but…"

"But what, Jordie?"

Jordie jumps up and down like he's riding a pogo stick.

"You're needed in the desert!"

Neville's hand goes straight to the statue in his pocket. He swallows hard.

"Are you saying what I think you're saying?"

Jordie nods wildly.

"You were right. Just where you said it would be. The palace gates. Beautifully preserved, considering. Superb in their artistry."

Neville covers his mouth with his palm. Big, like his grandfather's. He curls his hands into fists and looks up at the sky.

"We did it!" he says. "You hear me, Dad?" Tears stream from his eyes.

If I had eyes right now, I'm sure they would stream from mine.

"We leave tomorrow – before dawn," Jordie says, inhaling a good lungful. The air in Cairo, usually thick with pollution, is clearer today. Cleansed by a late northern wind. The kind that normally visits in the dead of winter.

"Why not tonight, after my lecture?"

"You need rest, Dr. Neville. And traveling the desert at night is dangerous – you know that. Not even the Arabs do it." Jordie slaps Neville on the shoulder. "Tomorrow will be a big day. Besides, if it is the oldest civilization ever discovered, it's been there for thousands of years. Hardly going to go away in the span of one night."

"The most ancient city in the world. The Palace City of the Rah'a." Neville says it like he still can't believe it. "Makes the pyramids of Giza look like a brand-new subdivision."

Cornelius Rodin Neville. Neil, to his wife. Neville to his friends. "That lucky bastard" to his envious colleagues. I do love him, but not like that. I've loved his family for generations and watch them every chance I get, which isn't nearly often enough.

"May I see it?" Jordie asks.

Neville nods, taking the statue out of his pocket and laying it in his assistant's outstretched hand. Jordie caresses its lines. He has long fingers for such a small man. "Not Sumerian after all. Much older. Your great-grandfather knew it all along, and they all laughed at him."

Neville paces along the pond, staring past the lily pads. The statue has been passed down in his family for over a hundred years, from archaeologist to archaeologist.

"Nin'ti are born for the love of only one, but to the

virtue of us all," he says. "That's what the ancients tell us, anyway; at least according to my grandfather. And each one has a divine quandary."

"A what?" Jordie asks.

"It's like a quest they must complete for the good of human kind. It's why they're born over and over again. I guess one life isn't nearly enough for that."

Jordie scratches his head, contemplating the statue. "I wonder if Nin'ti were destined for their fate or simply stumble upon it, the way one might chance upon a large fortune, or a killer on a darkened path?"

An ibis soars overhead, flapping its long, broad wings. Jordie jerks and looks up, crossing himself. From a distance, it does look an awful lot like the little figure he's holding.

"Nin'ti are a myth," Neville says. "Though a much older myth than anyone knew. Anyone but you, Granddad," he says again to the heavens.

"Uncover the past or die trying," Jordie says. "Isn't that your family motto?"

Neville laughs.

"Not literally. At least I hope not."

"But your father, and his father, and his father before that. They all died trying."

Neville looks at his assistant. He's quite tall, I realize. More so than his forefathers. At well over six feet, he towers over Jordie.

"I suppose they did."

Neville wraps his arms about his chest, contemplating those lily pads again. "You know, my grandfather thought he'd met one. A Nin'ti, I mean. My dad told me."

Jordie chuckles. "Ah, yes. But his people hailed from Senegal, and he was a creature of science and superstition. Like any archaeologist worth his salt, right?"

Neville nods, a big, white slice of a smile spreading across his face. "You oughta know, Jordie. Superstition is like a hereditary disease in your family."

Jordie feigns disgust. "But it skipped me!"

The north wind blows again. So light, like an infant's breath, but just strong enough to make Neville's shirt stick to his sweating torso. A strong back for an academic. He keeps fit to feed his addiction to the dig.

"You know, my ancestors traveled up from sub-Saharan Africa to Egypt to uncover the past. My great-grandfather came to America right after the First World War to study what he'd found. A partial tablet carved in a sophisticated language, one part word, and one part hieroglyph. Looked like visual music. Indecipherable. At least that's what everyone said. Everyone but him. There was this statue, of course. Little else. Only trinkets. A myth here and there. His endless talk about the dammed Nin'ti. It's all we had to go on."

Neville, with that faraway look on his face, turns his head to Jordie. Strong, straight line of a nose, irises like blackberries. It's the head of a raven.

"Granddad said you know a Nin'ti by their eyes. Those are supposed to be unusual, gem-like. Something out of a dream."

Jordie punches Neville's arm and starts to dance. "David Bowie was a Nin'ti! I knew it! Cha-cha-cha-changes!"

But Neville is paying no attention to the Bowie homage. He starts to pace again, cracking his knuckles. "He said being a Nin'ti was sort of like having a specific genetic trait – like being vulnerable to a certain illness. You might be a carrier, in which case nothing really happens and you live your one life. Or you may have a real susceptibility to becoming a Nin'ti, and all it takes is dying with another

Nin'ti to get that ball rolling, so to speak. Or dying at the hands of one."

Jordie stops his song and dance routine and studies his mentor.

"Do you believe?"

Neville cranes his neck and looks right at his assistant, blinking. "In Nin'ti? God, no. But I loved my grandfather. And I love old myths."

Emails are boring. Mine aren't. Cold Readers Club is a mini-magazine delivered to your inbox for free once a week, and it's one you're going to love. To join, go to www.victoriadoughertybooks.com and click "Get Your Cold On" at the top of the page.

Here's what readers are saying about Cold Readers Club:

"I look forward to your email every week and often read it twice! It's like getting a little magazine."—Peggy H.

"I know I'm not the only one in your *Cold Club*, but I always feel like you're writing something personal just for me."—Roger B.

"You share the most precious moments and write so beautifully. Now I have to read your fiction!"—Terry M.

VICTORIA DOUGHERTY writes about lovers, killers, curses and destinies. She is the author of the short story collection, *Welcome to the Hotel Yalta,* and the novels *The Bone Church, The Hungarian*, and *Savage Island.*

Her blog, Cold, featuring her essays on faith, family and writing has been singled out by WordPress, the blogging platform that hosts some 70 million blogs worldwide, as one of their top Recommended Blogs by writers and about writing.

Now available . . . *Breath*, an epic fantasy-romance series featuring the characters in Savage Island.

OTHER BOOKS BY VICTORIA DOUGHERTY

The Bone Church

Over 50,000 downloads, dozens of 5 star reviews!

In the surreal and paranoid underworld of wartime Prague, a man of God seeks the woman he once loved . . . Experience what readers have called "A deliciously dark tale" . . . "Hauntingly real" . . . and "A beautifully written literary thriller."

The Hungarian

An heiress who can't seem to keep her legs closed. A Russian plan for dominating the space race. An assassin with a penchant for rich food and sadistic murder. When you're alone in the cold, passion and betrayal are commodities and love hangs on by an icy thread . . .

Here's what readers are saying:

"A page turner that will keep you reading long into the night! Once again, Victoria Dougherty, an incredibly gifted writer, pulls the reader into a journey through a grisly web of deceit, betrayal, torture, passion, and espionage that spans from Greece to Russia, Europe and the Middle East during the late '50's."—Honeyplh

"The plot line is so enthralling that as I neared the end of the book I got up and made myself a cup of coffee, wanting to delay the finish. And at the final words, I smiled."—T.W. Dittmer

Available exclusively on Amazon!

IF YOU LOVED SAVAGE ISLAND, please leave a review on Goodreads or any of your favorite platforms. It doesn't have to be long, just speak from your heart. Reviews are the lifeblood of an author. Not only do they let us know how you feel about our work, but they trigger the complicated algorithms that help make our books visible to readers. Without them, readers will literally not know our books exist.

Thank you.

Made in the USA
Monee, IL
25 April 2023

413295dd-c7fa-4af3-b049-393fba4c0b74R01